Burn Before Reading

Tina Kakadelis

Carly Allen is finishing up her senior year of high school. After a rough break-up at the beginning of the year, she's ready to move on and leave her hometown in the dust. The only problem? She still hasn't heard back from any of the colleges she applied to. As the end of the year approaches, will Carly be able to figure out her future in time? Throw in a new crush, a moderately successful high school jam band, and a sarcastic freshman to tutor, and it'll be a miracle if she makes it to graduation alive.

To my fifteen-year-old self: I hope this is the book you were looking for all those years ago.

P.S. You're old now. Your hip pops when you get out of bed. Why'd you let this happen?

1

It's My Party
by Lesley Gore

It's going to be an awful party and Annie promises she'll buy me dinner at the Towson Diner after it's over, but I'm not budging. Annie's been talking to a boy on her debate team for the better part of a year and they've finally decided to actually hang out in public. Gasp. Outside of school. However, when it comes to dating and boys, Annie's an endearing, but decisively bumbling mess, so I'm being bribed to go along. I'd already been invited by Cameron, who was throwing the party, but I said no because I was six seasons deep into *Gilmore Girls*. The plan was to finish it by this Sunday. Tragically, for me at least, Annie has decided this is the perfect weekend for a date.

"I just don't understand why it's so important for me to chaperone this date of yours," I grumble as Annie tosses outfits around me on the bed.

"You aren't chaperoning, Carly. Don't be so dramatic," she says as she holds up a blue striped dress and looks at herself in the mirror. "You'll just be observing from a distance. You know, so we can go over every second in excruciating detail after."

I slam my head on my computer. "Oh my god."

"It won't be that bad," Annie consoles me as she sits on the edge of the bed. "Besides, I trust you and I need you! This is the closest thing I've had to a date in a very long time."

"Me too."

"Can it, Carly. I'm being serious."

I sit up and study Annie. She's standing there twirling her hair between her fingers and tugging on her dress. "Hey, it'll be just fine. This guy obviously likes you, so you have nothing to worry about."

She rolls her eyes. "But, like, what if this is all some dumb *She's All That* thing? What if they're just planning to dump a bucket of blood on me?"

I laugh. "I think you've got your movies mixed up. And besides, don't Rachael Leigh Cook and Freddie Prinze Jr. end up together in the end?"

"Yeah, you're right. And the blood girl goes apeshit on the entire school, so I guess it doesn't matter."

"Beautiful. It's settled then. I'll continue to watch Alexis Bledel get more attractive as the seasons pass and you'll have a wonderful time tonight with Todd, the debate boy," I say, turning back over onto my stomach.

"Oh, no, you're not getting off that easily," Annie says, snapping my laptop closed and grabbing it from me.

"Hey!"

"Look, Carly, I get that you're still kind of moping about Emma, but she's a bitch and it's over. So put on something cute and we'll find you a nice girl."

"That's quite alright," I say, reaching for my laptop. "Dying alone is gaining a certain appeal."

Annie smacks my arm away. "Get your ass out of bed, superstar."

****

For most of my life, I thought of myself as a happy person. I was good at just rolling with the punches. Things, as a whole, were unequivocally fine. Unfortunately, all that changed when Emma came along. Pretty girls have a way of changing everything.

She was a barista. How absolutely adorable, right? I'd always wanted to date a barista because I thought free coffee would be the ultimate perk. Get it? Perk? Coffee? I'm sorry, I hoped humor would dull my pain.

Coffee was probably the best, most functional aspect of our relationship. I still have bags stockpiled from our time together. Emma got a free pound of coffee every week, but she didn't drink coffee, so they were all mine. A barista who didn't drink coffee. Yeah. It should've been my first red flag, but I was hopelessly blinded by her smile and completely intoxicated by the smell of freshly ground coffee.

It wasn't like we were glaringly dysfunctional from the get-go. That would've been too easy. No, it was a steady build. Red flag after red flag until I was helpless, my white flag invisible and indistinguishable from the sea I was drowning in.

I noticed her each time I went to the Starbucks across town. Because I'm a terrible human and I waste money I should be saving for college on frivolous things, I go to Starbucks regularly, but Emma didn't work at my usual one. She worked at the one closer to Annie's house. My visits began to increase once I noticed just how cute she looked in her little black polo shirt and baseball cap. She made the first move, though, when she put a heart next to my name on the cup. I checked each of my friends' cups, but they were without that cute little heart. It took a week for me to find the courage to even consider asking her out.

"Always give your number," Annie had said. "It's kind of a courtesy. Like now she can be very flattered, but not interested, and ignore you forever. Or she can text you the second she goes on break. It's really win-win."

Annie likes calling situations win-win. It gives her a false sense of confidence and an aura of expertise on the subject when, in reality, she's a frightened little meerkat if there's an opportunity for her to take her own advice. (See: my current predicament.)

No thanks to Annie's attempts at pep talks, I did ask this pretty coffee girl out. I walked into her Starbucks one afternoon and ordered the cheapest thing I could find from the boy at the register. He wrote my name (minus the heart) on the cup and passed it down the line to her. I had no intention of drinking whatever it was I'd just ordered. My stomach felt like it was training for the Olympic gymnastics team. Sprinting, flipping, jumping.

Turns out I ordered a single shot of espresso. Emma kept that cup as long as we dated. I expect it's in a landfill now. No, she probably recycled it. That was at least one thing she had going for her.

Emma quickly made my one shot of espresso, and it occurred to me that in order for my plan to actually work, I should've ordered something slightly more complex. She called my name, and I responded with a sheepish grin and a raised arm. She smiled at me and I swore the rest of the world melted away just for that instant.

"Mixing it up today, I see," she said, pushing my drink across the bar.

I smiled. "Variety's the spice of life, you know."

Shit, that was so stupid.

"Have a good day, Carly," Emma said as the register boy passed her another cup.

I nodded, and as she started working on the next drink, I pulled out the Sharpie I'd bought just for this moment. Quickly scrawling my phone number under my name, I wrote "We should get coffee someplace you don't have to make it."

At the time, I was quite proud of that line. Only a little later did I find out she's an utter fool with no taste for coffee. What kind of barista doesn't drink coffee? I'm sorry I keep bringing that up, but, like, come on. It's weird. What is she gaining from this experience? I know what you're thinking. "Slow down, Carly, maybe she drinks tea." Yeah, no she doesn't. So I think my outrage is justified.

"Steve? Your iced coffee," Emma called, not even waiting for him to pick it up before she went about busying herself cleaning.

Now or never.

"Hey, um, there was something wrong with my drink."

She looked up, confused. "It's just a shot of espresso. What could possibly be wrong with it?"

I knew I should've ordered something more complicated. "Well, uh, I ordered a double, but this is just a single," I said, putting the cup down and sliding it back to her.

"Let me look at it," she said.

I think this is my favorite memory of our relationship. Watching Emma read the note and seeing the tentative grin sneak across her face. She looked so sweet then, before everything bad happened. Sometimes I wish relationships ended there. In that sweet moment, still all wrapped up like a Christmas present, filled with wonder and so delicately bound. No fights or anything to mess it up, just feeling wanted in the simplest way. In that moment, her fingers tracing over my words, smiling like she was reading Shakespeare, I did want her.

She looked up. "It's a damn shame I don't like coffee."

2

You Give Love a Bad Name
by Bon Jovi

Emma went to a high school down the road from mine, so our relationship lived in skipped periods and evenings at each other's house, usually under the pretense of studying. Oh, man, how did we get away with that? Maybe our parents just didn't care because we were already immune to teen pregnancy. Whatever the case, it was blissful. We made out in my car, her car, my room, her room, the back row of empty Friday afternoon movie theatres, football fields at two a.m., under football bleachers at eleven a.m., in the changing room at T.J. Maxx, and the list goes on. I believe the two most creative groups of people are stoners in need of bongs and teenagers who want to make out.

So that was the beginning, around November of our junior year. Summer wasn't much different. We fell into a lazy rhythm of me working at my record store job from nine to three while Emma had the opening Starbucks shift. Then we'd drive out to the pool her parents belonged to.

She'd lie on her towel, bikini top unclipped, trying to get the perfect tan, while I attempted to play basketball. Every once in a while, I'd lie down next to her, help reapply sunscreen, and steal a kiss or two before going back to the game. When it was finally dark out, we'd head to the park and make out until we couldn't feel our lips anymore under the starry summer sky. Wash, rinse, repeat, all summer long.

I didn't see Annie until mid-July, when she showed up on my porch at 7:30 in the morning and went off on me for abandoning her for Emma. She talked all about how inconsiderate I was being, and she was right. The only person I ever saw was Emma. I was with my parents so infrequently that it took me almost two weeks to notice my dad had shaved his head. It's not even like he had a partially shaved head to begin with. No, my dad had gone from straight-up shoulder length hippie hair to Telly Savalas.

I figured Annie's comments were reasonable, mostly because they genuinely were. Emma and I didn't have any concrete plans, so I shot her a quick text saying I was going to spend the day with Annie. No harm, no foul, I thought. This would turn out to be the first of many, many, many fights. Emma went off on me, saying what an awful person I was because I was quote unquote abandoning her like this, the whole nine million yards. It went on like that for a good while.

Now I know what you're thinking. Carly, if this girl's a

nutcase, and she so clearly is, why did you continue to date her? Well, fine, reasonable human, I'll tell you. 1. She's hot and we're all a little (a lot) bit shallow in high school. 2. Honestly, it didn't seem like that big an issue. 3. I was kind of flattered that she liked me so much she wanted to spend all her time with me. In the infinite wisdom I have now, I see the error of my ways, but I'd also like to refer you back to reason #1.

And thus began the horrible, burning, dumpster tailspin of the last few months of our relationship. We fought almost every day over the dumbest things. Maybe it was an abandoned McDonald's wrapper in my backseat or the time I mentioned how I wanted a dog and she considered the simple desire to want a dog to be monumentally inconsiderate because she's allergic. Of course, my hanging out with Annie didn't help. To spite me, Emma started spending time with this new, very obviously gay girl on her soccer team who wore her crush on Emma proudly on her sleeve. It didn't bother me because I didn't believe she'd actually cheat on me. Spoiler: I should not enter a career in which my success relies on my ability to read people's character.

I don't know how long they were sneaking around behind my back. We still had our summer rhythm, but I spent weekends with Annie and Emma hung out with Zoe, the soccer girl. We were shockingly still together when our senior year started, and I suspect this is when their secret trysts really amped up.

I heard it through the grapevine, like most people do. Despite what The CW wants you to believe, I feel like most people come across cheating in simple ways. Never as outright and boisterous as walking in on someone mid-bang sesh. Since our two schools were so close, lots of kids had a foot in both pools. When I first heard murmurings of Emma and Zoe, I shrugged it off. We hadn't been in a fight in a while, but that probably should've been the biggest red flag of all. Eventually, the rumors piled up and I finally confronted her, which, as I'm sure you can guess, turned out to be a truly terrible plan. We broke up. Not sure who technically broke up with who, but it was a knock-down drag-out fight for the ages.

At first, I was stoked. It felt like a weight had been lifted off my shoulders. I went to parties and made out with every girl I could find. I was able to ride that ignorant wave until about mid-December. I was walking through Urban Outfitters and saw a book with pigs in party hats on the cover. I picked it up and absentmindedly thought how much Emma would like it because she weirdly loves pigs. My brain slowly caught up with that runaway thought and tried to backpedal, but it was too late. I felt this tsunami wash over me. Every ounce of sadness I'd kept at bay for three months was suddenly rolling full force right at me.

I remember dropping the book and trying to walk as calmly as I could to my car. When I got there, I turned it on and just let the heat blast over me. I held it together until Taylor Swift's *All Too Well* started playing on the radio. I could be in the happiest mood in the world and I'd still be crying by the end of that song. I'm not ashamed about that. Anyone with a heart cries listening to that song.

Sobbing in the car in the parking lot is the worst because you've got all these people walking past trying to find their own car. God forbid they mistake your car for theirs and walk up to the driver's window and there you are, just weeping uncontrollably.

Of course, once the tsunami started, I was totally consumed by Emma. I checked all her social media accounts and saw she and that Zoe girl had started dating like a week and a half after we broke up. Stupid Emma and those stupidly cute pictures of them at a pumpkin patch and them dressed up as Ruby Rose's character and Piper Chapman for Halloween. Coincidentally, I dressed up as Alex Vause that year, but I'm still trying really hard not to read too much into that.

I couldn't stop. I became obsessed with their relationship. When I'd be trying to fall asleep is when all the questions really came at me. What about Zoe was better than me? Was she cuter? A better kisser? Smarter? Funnier? What was it? Was I just plain and simple not good enough for Emma? I got real existential for a while. I still can't get it out of the back of my mind. Whenever I talk to a pretty girl, there's a little voice that says "You weren't good enough for Emma, so what makes you think you could possibly be good enough for this girl?" You know, just all-around healthy, productive thoughts.

The fact that the relationship was garbage doesn't mean it was any less fundamentally heartbreaking when it ended. I'm a Bruce Springsteen girl through and through, but Taylor Swift understands the human condition so well. She's had her heart broken once or twice or four hundred times, that's for sure. For a long time, Annie would come over and find me lying on the ground with a sleeve of Oreos and Taylor Swift's *Red* on the record player. It would be so much easier to simply pull up a cry-your-eyes-out playlist on Spotify, but I'm a pretentious douchebag and so is Taylor Swift because her music isn't there.

How dumb is it that we romanticize record players in times of heartbreak? All you want to do is lie there and wallow and do absolutely nothing, but record players demand attention. Otherwise, the needle will slide off the record and you'll be left with silence, and we all know that's entirely too terrifying. I don't even know the last time I allowed the world around me to be completely silent.

So the days passed with Taylor Swift and Oreos, lazily watching HGTV reruns as if I was actually renovating a house. I hate the fake drama they add in those shows. Oh, no, a mysterious water leak means the hardwood floors are damaged beyond repair. The people are never concerned. They're just like, yep, $20,000 for new hardwood floors sounds reasonable. As casually as you'd pay $3 for some coffee. As casually as some people apparently can rip out someone else's heart and send it through a wood chipper.

I'm sure it couldn't have been really real love. She was my first love, but it wasn't love. Geez, that makes no sense. I cared about her deeply, I'm sure of that, but it wasn't love. At least, I hope that's not what I have to look forward to. There was never that pure, sustained electricity that I think love is. She was a possibility that never reached its full potential. The only thing getting me through this shit show is that possibilities are endless. All of them smiling and brimming with promises and futures of love. Sunny mornings in your button-down shirt, hair all sleepy wild. Sunday evenings with wind whipping through your hair, top down, and the sun setting like caramel. Heart alive and filled with tiny singing Disney woodland creatures. The spectacularness of the world so overwhelmingly roaring with the rising moon. I could live forever in that magic hour. The time of caramel sunsets swirled with the beginnings of a dark chocolate night and a pretty girl in the passenger seat in it for the long haul.

Wow. Sorry. I'm getting ahead of myself.

I think that's when all the greats must've written their best songs, though. *Thunder Road, Free Fallin', Faithfully, Going to California.* I mean, I can just picture Springsteen sitting on the hood of an old Chevy, guitar in hand, dreaming far beyond the sunsets of Asbury Park. Making music to run away to. Man, these guys must've loved some real, honest-to-goodness babes. But I guess anyone could break your heart on evenings like those.

So that brings us to today. Annie begging me to go to this stupid party and me still attempting to get out of it. Even I know a losing battle when I see one.

"Carly, it's time! Come on, let's go!" I can hear the enthusiasm in her voice. She's just so excited about this boy. I'm happy for her. Todd and I have had a few classes together through the years. He laughs at my jokes about our teachers. In my book, that makes for a pretty solid dude.

I give my closet a once-over and start to throw on any old t-shirt. No. You know what? I'm going to take Annie's advice for the first time in my life and I'm going to look damn cute for this stupid party. I pull out a short-sleeve button-up shirt my mom bought me last week that still has the tags on it. She said it was lesbian geek chic. I really need to take *People* magazine away from her.

So, yeah. Emma's not the only lesbian in Towson and I look pretty adorable in my new lesbian geek chic shirt. I pull on black pants, my favorite brown boots, and run my hands through my hair about fifty times. Annie and I once decorated my mirror with alphabet stickers to spell out "What Would Harry Styles Do?" Well, I think he'd be pretty proud of me tonight.

"Nuh-uh, go back upstairs and put on a brown belt," Annie says as I make my way into the kitchen.

"What are you talking about?" I ask, looking down at my waist.

She shakes her head. "You can only wear brown shoes and black pants if your belt matches your shoes."

"Ah, yes, but I don't have a belt on," I say as I steal a chip from the salsa and chips she's set out.

"Yes, and yet you have shoes on. Funny. Now go," she insists, pointing back upstairs.

I huff and stomp back up to my room.

"At least your butt looks great in those pants," Annie calls after me.

3

I've Just Seen a Face
by The Beatles

We arrive at the party fashionably late, no thanks to Annie. She was dead set on getting there at exactly the suggested start time, but I held strong. Some of us do have a reputation to uphold. I suspect she only wanted to be there early to maximize her time with Todd. Turns out I'm 1,000,000% correct, because the second we step through the doors, she pulls me along to try and find him. Not that I'm shocked by this outcome in the slightest.

"Todd! There you are!" Annie exclaims. Her huge smile gives everything away. It's gross.

"Hey, I was wondering when you were gonna get here. I've been here since 9:00," he adds sheepishly, but returns her smile.

Dear god. He got here right on time. I'm sure he must've made awkward small talk with Mr. and Mrs. Cameron's Parents. Annie shoots me an I-told-you-so look, but I just do her signature eye roll. They're perfect for each other.

I miss having a crush. Someone who would make me want to go to school or look forward to going to some meaningless party. I miss having butterflies in my stomach about a person. It just adds a little something extra to life, you know? Life's already a pretty solid box of chocolates, but a crush is like the sparkly ribbon on the box. It's not necessary, but it makes everything just a little nicer, neater. Makes you excited for what's to come. Instead of having that nervous energy, I'm aimlessly wandering around this party.

My phone feels warm in my pocket. I could call Emma. I used to smile at her the same way I saw Annie smile tonight. I don't miss Emma. I miss having someone on my team like Emma. I could call her, though. I could call her right now and I'm almost positive she'd be up for another go at this.

No, no, no.

I don't want to do that. I want another chance, but not with her. I want the nervousness Annie had tonight. I want to change my outfit ten times before I go out. I want to be self-conscious about how my breath smells. I want to spend my life in a tomato red blush-filled state of bliss. I want all of those things with a new person. Sadly, at this point, I don't even have anyone on my mind. High school's almost over, though, so no point in trying to find anything serious.

Looks like third wheeling is all I have in the cards for the foreseeable future.

After a quick pit stop in the bathroom, I step outside to find a bottle of water. I'm the designated driver tonight since I'm banking on Annie needing more than a little liquid courage to get her through the evening. On the patio, there are kids laughing and drinking. It's very mundane, like every party I've been to in the last four years. It seems even the impending end of our known world can't really change high schoolers all that much.

I see some friends kicking around a soccer ball while trying to angle their cups so they don't lose any beer. Theatre kids and athletes. I love these people. I know them all intimately. Take Luke Williams. Junior. Only freshman to make starting varsity baseball. Held back a year for trying to sabotage the school musical by streaking. He loves birds. Like adores them. Spends weekends in the state park taking pictures of them and documenting their movements. He's part of some national bird organization. Laughing at some dumb joke he made is Madison Hope. She's going to Vanderbilt for pre-law. No one knows yet. She's still saying she's trying to narrow it down, but she's known since she got the acceptance letter weeks ago. I overheard her on the phone with her mom during lunch. She made me promise not to tell because her best friend Mollie Fae didn't get in.

Speaking of Mollie Fae, I see her playing beer pong in

the yard. We don't really know each other. Once upon a time, we were in an English class together for a day before her schedule got switched. She moved here from Arizona freshman year, and despite her high school royalty status, her dating life was never widely publicized. Maybe the gossip just didn't make it to me, but I never heard about Mollie Fae dating anyone. Which is just absurd.

We're on opposite sides of the social hierarchy, both well-known in our own right, but she's more classically popular. You know, the beautiful girl with the charming, bubbly personality. Seemingly untouchable. Honest to goodness high school royalty. That's Mollie Fae. A girl so great you have to say her full name. I, on the other hand, am popular without that sense of royalty. A kind of popularity achieved by being unthreatening and nice to everyone in school. Oh, and good hair. Having good hair has really helped out.

Speaking of good hair, Mollie Fae is walking over to me and I feel my palms start to sweat. Be cool, Carly. You've talked to pretty girls before. And yet, the closer she gets the more I'm positive I've never talked to a girl like her before.

I coax my face into what I'm praying isn't a serial killer smile. "Hey."

The smile she beams at me is effortless. "Hi."

"Having fun?" I ask.

"Yeah, I'm playing beer pong. Winning, actually. But

the, uh, ball is between your feet," she responds, pointing down.

"Oh, yeah. Sorry, I didn't notice."

We both go to grab the ball, but Mollie's faster and something sharp on the back of her head slams hard into my eye. She jumps back with a yelp and holds the back of her head. Meanwhile, I'm still partially hunched over, seeing stars.

"Holy hell, you've got a really solid head." Smooth, Carly Allen. Smooth as expired milk.

She looks up. "Oh, no. Did my hairclip hit your eye?" She pulls my face close to take a look, and all I can see are her beautiful green eyes.

"So that's what that was. It stabbed me, but I think I'm okay."

"Your eye is closed."

"Oh," I say. "I hadn't noticed. I thought this was how things always looked."

"Can you try to open it?" she asks, lightly touching my eyebrow.

"Oh, definitely no. I think I need some ice."

"Come on, I'll lead you there," Mollie says, dropping the ball. I hear it bounce away.

"What about your beer pong champion status?"

"There'll be other parties," she answers, tugging me into the kitchen.

The kitchen lights are hazy, and I steady myself by leaning on the counter as Mollie opens the freezer door. She mutters something I can't understand.

"What's wrong?"

"Cameron must've used all the ice for the punch."

"There's probably some in the pool house freezer," I offer.

"Onward!" Mollie says, grabbing my hand.

We're back outside again and I think my eye is starting to be fine, but I don't want to tell her that. Right now I'd blindly follow Mollie to the edge of the earth, and I barely know her. Apparently I'm like a human dodo bird when it comes to pretty girls.

"Watch your step," she says.

My toe hits the lip of the sliding glass door Mollie just warned me about. I stumble forward, but she catches me before I bite it hard.

"Didn't you hear me?" she laughs. "I thought when one sense gets messed up the other ones get stronger."

"I don't think it's instantaneous," I say, blinking a few times. "Besides, I think my eye's okay."

The first thing I can somewhat clearly make out is Mollie grimacing.

"What's wrong?"

"Your eye isn't red or bleeding or anything, but it looks like you got clocked by someone," she says, moving closer to inspect the damage. I remember the copious amounts of garlic in the salsa I ate with Annie before I arrived and hold my breath.

"Yeah, we should definitely get you some ice," she says.

"You know I'm going to have to explain this to my parents. They'll think I'm in some weird underground fight club."

She whips around. "You can't talk about Fight Club."

"I'm serious," I say, laughing anyway.

"What? They won't believe you got head-butted by a random girl at a party?" Mollie questions as she wraps some ice in a dish towel.

"You're not random. I remember you." It's out of my mouth before I can stop myself.

"You remember me, huh?" she asks, handing me the ice.

I clear my throat and rest the ice on my eye. "I mean, yeah. You transferred here. Freshman year?"

"You do have a good memory. Carly, right?"

"How'd you remember that?" I ask incredulously.

She shrugs. "Good with faces, I guess."

I could be hallucinating, or hazy from getting whacked in the face by a butterfly hairclip, but I'd bet the only three dollars in my wallet that she's blushing.

"That's something we have in common, Mollie Fae," I say.

"I guess it is, Carly Allen," she responds. "It also answers the concussion concern." She hops onto the countertop.

"Definitely not concussed, but I feel like an eye patch is in my future," I laugh.

"Lemme see," she says. "Oh, yeah, that's not good. And we have senior photos on Monday. I am so, so sorry."

"It's okay. It'll be a fun story to tell my kids one day. Everyone else will have a boring photo and there I'll be, smiling with a black eye."

"Are you going to make yourself into a hero?" she asks.

"Yeah, my kids will never know the truth. I'll tell them I beat up someone who was stealing candy from a kid. You have to promise to take it to your grave, though."

"Oh, I do?" she questions, crossing her arms.

"Of course. I can't live with the fear of you showing up on my doorstep one day and exposing me as a liar. My kids would never let me live that down."

She laughs loudly. "Okay, whatever you say, hero."

****

Annie walked into the pool house a little while later and found us sitting on the countertop. She swears we were no more than a centimeter apart, but I think she's got love-drunk, rose-colored glasses on. Apparently, things are going swimmingly with Todd. All they did was hold hands, and

Annie's utterly through the roof. She might spontaneously combust when they kiss. It's sweet, and the two of us can't stop smiling at each other across the table at the diner. She's as excited for me as she is for herself, but I still think it's nothing.

"Mollie was basically sitting on your lap, Carly," Annie says, dipping a fry into her milkshake while I feign revulsion.

"It was not that big a deal. We were just talking. It's really not this big, dramatic thing you're making it out to be. You and I sit next to each other all the time. I sit next to people all the time."

She contemplates this for just the smallest fraction of a second. "Yes, but you and I have been friends since we were in kindergarten. This girl barely has any idea who you are, and she's getting close and cozy. Not that it looked like you minded."

"But still," I say, slumping down in the booth, "I don't think this is something we need to over-analyze."

"Oh, okay, so next time we hang out, I'm just going to sit real close to you and gaze longingly into your eyes," Annie teases. "Like, usually I'm the romantically incompetent one, but even I could see that girl was drooling. And all you can say is 'that's just what friends do.' Sorry, but no."

I lean down and put my head on the table. "Don't tell

me this. My crush is already growing exponentially."

"I knew it!" Annie yells, startling the few other patrons in the restaurant. She smiles at them apologetically while I start hitting my head on the table.

"You sure know how to pick 'em, Carly. She's a cutie," Annie says, and I don't even need to look up to see that stupid look on her face. So rude. It's the same one she had when I came out to her years ago and she asked me if it was because of Stella Carraway. Which, I mean it totally was, but still, rude.

"You literally said no words to this girl," I say, without lifting my head at all.

"Yeah, but she has a nice smile and I could tell she was a sweetheart," Annie replies, almost wistfully. I'm pretty sure her mind has drifted back to Todd. There's no way she gleaned all this from the two seconds when she stormed into the pool house and pulled me off the countertop without so much as a glance in Mollie's direction.

"You're such a sap. I see that smile," Annie says as she tousles my hair.

I look up. "I'm so, so pathetic it's insane."

"Honestly? I've always thought it was very sweet the way you get about a girl you like." I scoff at her comment. "Stop it. I'm being serious. I see the way you get all nervous and tongue-tied around these girls you have crushes on and it's so refreshing. That's how people should like each other.

Very simply, very, just, you know, easy! I don't think you give yourself enough credit. You're cute and you're honest. Own it."

"Thanks, Mom."

"Don't be an ass. I'm not just being nice to you. Carly, you're a sweetheart and you need to recognize that girls are going to notice that and like it. Just go out on a limb and ask her out or something."

I shake my head. "No, not yet. I just, I don't know, I just want to make sure it's legit, okay?"

"Not every girl's as bad as Emma."

"And not everybody's as cool as Todd."

"Touché." Annie raises her glass. "Although I will say, your eye is going to look so terrible for picture day."

4

Just What I Needed
by The Cars

I walk down the stairs the next morning to what appears to be an empty house. I'm hoping to avoid the inevitable parental inquisition until dinnertime. The swelling did not go down overnight, so it looks like I will in fact take my picture tomorrow with a massive black eye.

"Whoa-ho-oh, look at the shiner on you, kiddo," my dad says from the recliner.

"Geez, Dad! Why are you sitting there like some evil movie villain?"

"Why are you fighting with people?"

"It wasn't a fight. I just ran into this girl. It's not a big deal," I mumble.

"It's fine. No sweat. I got into some fights in my day," Dad says wistfully.

"Did you now? Seems to go against the hippie peace and love mentality you pride yourself on," I say, grabbing a box of Triscuits from the kitchen and taking a seat on the couch back in the living room.

He waves me off. "I'm talking way before that."

Just then, my mom walks through the door, sees my black eye, and dramatically drops all her grocery bags.

"Carly Allen! What on earth happened?"

As you can see, my parents are wildly different. My father's a hippie who would have gone to Woodstock, has long hair, and definitely smoked pot back in the day. My mother, on the other hand, could probably tell you the chemical makeup of marijuana, but has never actually tried it herself. She has a Ph.D. in some kind of biology that I can't even pretend to understand; big on answers and steps and hypotheses. My dad's more go with the flow, do whatever you want, just don't get arrested unless it's for a really good cause.

"It's not a big deal, Mom. Your husband said he used to fight people all the time."

"You got into a fight?"

"I mean, no, but throwing Dad under the bus seemed like a solid defense," I mutter.

"Then what did happen?"

"Nothing weird or anything to worry about. This girl and I just ran into each other at the party I went to last night. I'm fine, she's fine, everything's fine."

The sound of the doorbell distracts my mother. The three of us stare at each other, clearly finding it difficult to move on from my shiner.

"Is Annie coming over?" Mom asks.

"Nope."

"I'm not answering it," Dad says, reclining further.

My mom sighs and opens the door. She starts to offer a greeting, but no one's there.

"Is ding dong ditch a thing people still do?" I ask.

"There's a box here," my mom says.

That instantly makes Dad invested in what's going on at the front door. Me too, if I'm honest about it.

"It looks like a cake box," Dad says, getting out of his comfy chair and joining Mom by the door.

"I think that's exactly what it is," Mom replies.

"Where's it from?" I ask, walking over to them.

"You can see as well as I can that there aren't any markings," Mom answers. With a little bit of sass, I might add.

"Are you spies? Like *Spy Kids* spies?" I ask.

"We're not kids," Dad responds.

"No, I know. The kids are only spies because they have to save their actual spy parents from these evil human thumb things," I explain. I shake my head. "Never mind. It's not worth explaining it to you."

"I imagine the evil human thumb things are the beginning of a long list of scientific inaccuracies in that movie," my mom states.

"Dunno, hon. Those thumb things sound pretty realistic given the current state of America's medical system. Thanks, Obama," Dad says, elbowing me in the side.

"What? No, Dad, you literally campaigned for Obama. We still have an Obama '08 sign in our front yard. We're a pro-Obama household. I don't think you get to say things like that."

"It's a joke, Carly. Irony. Kids these days always say 'Thanks, Obama' as a joke. Shouldn't you know that? Even I know that."

I laugh. "Do you have a subscription to Kids These Days: How to Remain Hip When What You Really Need Is to Get Your Hip Replaced?"

"Not really your best comeback."

I sigh. "It sounded a lot snappier in my head."

"Delivery needs work."

"Are you two finished bickering?" my mom interrupts. "There's possibly a cake here that I'd like to open."

"Yeah, yeah, open it!" I say.

My mom opens the box and it's a beautiful cake. Beautiful in the sense that it's from the best bakery in town. Graul's is technically a grocery store, but their bakery is unbeatable. We've gotten birthday and anniversary cakes from there for as long as I can remember. In fact, we're such huge fans of their cakes that a few years ago we started making up celebrations just so we could order a cake. Fake birthdays for fake family members, half-birthdays, monthiversaries for my parents' marriage, you name it. When I came home from a trip to Mexico with Annie's family without getting Montezuma's revenge, my parents got me a cake. When I had a huge cut that got infected, we celebrated its healing with a cake that said Glad You Survived Necrotizing Fasciitis. I wonder what the cake decorators think of us.

It looks like this cake is no different. It says Sorry For Head-Butting Your Daughter. I grin when I read it. The sound of a car sputtering to life comes from across the street, and I look over to see an old, beat-up, yellow Beetle. The window's down and I recognize Mollie instantly, her long hair blowing in the wind. I catch her eye, then she smiles and slides her sunglasses off the top of her head before making her getaway.

"Someone head-butted you?" Mom asks.

I look over at her. "Yeah. I told you I ran into someone. That's what this is all about," I say, pointing to my eye.

"So you did get into a fight," Dad says.

"No, it was an accidental head-butting. We bumped into each other is all," I say, looking back down at the cake. I can't stop reading the words.

Dad shrugs. "Good enough for me."

He takes the cake and starts to walk into the kitchen. My mom catches the dreamy smile plastered on my face and I wipe it away quickly. She studies me for a second, eyes squinting ever so slightly, before following Dad into the kitchen.

I pull out my phone and open the Facebook app. In the brief period of a little more than twelve hours since Mollie and I re-met, I've looked at her profile an embarrassing number of times. For the most part, she keeps everything private, which I find very disappointing. My finger hovers over the Add as Friend button. It's not weird to add her, right? I mean, she hand-delivered me a cake. That's weird. If she can bring me a cake, I can be her Internet acquaintance.

Right?

Right.

I hit the Friend Request button, close the app, and shut off my phone. Classic Carly Allen avoidance technique. I walk into the kitchen and my mom passes me a plate of cake. Just as I'm about to take my first bite, my phone buzzes.

Mollie Fae has accepted your Friend Request.

That stupid, dreamy smile of mine finds its way back. I unlock my phone and open Facebook again. There's the little red notification bubble making me feel way giddier than it should. I click on Mollie's profile and start typing a comment on her wall. Do people even do that anymore? Should I be this invested in what's considered acceptable on social media? Somebody save me from myself.

> Loved the cake, but so much for taking this to our graves

Her response comes as I'm eating a pastel-colored icing flower from the top of the cake.

> You're the one who put the damning evidence on social media. I just wrote it on a cake. That way, the evidence is destroyed when you eat it ☺

I spend the rest of the day feeling like I could walk on water.

5

(What a) Wonderful World
by Sam Cooke

On Monday morning, my mom comes bursting into my room. Apparently she wants to check on the healing process of my injury and can't wait until my usual wake-up time to do it. I've already accepted the fact that I'll have a black eye immortalized for all eternity in my senior photo. Clearly, my mother has not. The thought of sending her relatives a less-than-perfect senior picture may be too much for her to handle. As a result, I'm being forcibly dragged into the bathroom before the sun has even risen.

"Mom, it's just a black eye, who cares?" I grumble, wiping the sleep from my eyes.

"Your grandmother, that's who," Mom responds, pulling makeup out of her bag.

"Nuh-uh. I don't wear make-up and I'm not starting today," I pout. No, I'm not above pouting. Desperate times, y'know?

"Carly, just a little bit of makeup to cover up this

monstrosity."

"Monstrosity? How dare you speak to your only child like that!" I exclaim.

Mom sighs. "You're really not going to make this easy, are you?"

"Nope."

She studies my face for a moment. "I guess it's better than yesterday."

"See? And it'll be a better story. I mean, any old schmuck can have a perfect senior photo. This'll make it fun."

She laughs lightly. "You really are your father's daughter."

"Eh, I haven't seen the proof."

"Have you decided what you're wearing for the picture?" Mom asks.

"Don't need to. They give you this weird smock that makes it look like you're wearing a dress. I'm good," I respond, walking out of the bathroom.

"At least brush your hair!"

****

I remember to brush my hair as I'm waiting in line to have my picture taken. I guess, technically, it's Annie who reminds me.

"I really like the Albert Einstein look you've got going

on," she says.

I reach up to touch my hair. "Shit."

"Between that and the black eye, you've just guaranteed yourself a place in a BuzzFeed article about most ridiculous school photos."

"Thank you for your support."

"Oh, things just keep getting better," Annie says. "Look who's in charge of helping with the smocks."

I can guess who it's going to be just based on Annie's tone. As I expect, it's Mollie Fae, looking beautiful as ever with hair that's definitely been brushed. I wonder what it's like to show up on picture day with brushed hair and clothes without coffee stains.

"Annie, I need you to fix me," I plead.

"That's quite the undertaking," she says.

"Just fix my hair, please."

Annie starts combing her hands through my hair and pressing sections down in an attempt to make me look decent. The line continues to move forward and I'm worried we don't have enough time. Never in my life have I been this nervous about picture day. We're almost at the front, but Mollie still hasn't caught sight of us.

"How's it coming up there?" I ask.

"Better. I think. Well, it certainly doesn't look styled, maybe more like you got struck by lightning on purpose," Annie responds.

"Good enough for me," I say, just as we move again, making us next in line for the photographer.

"Here you go. For your senior quote," Mollie says, turning around. "Oh! Hey! I was wondering when you'd show up."

I laugh awkwardly because my brain short-circuited when Mollie said she was wondering about me.

"Yeah, we're in Mr. Hall's English class on the fourth floor, so I think we're one of the last ones," Annie says, rescuing me.

"He might actually be the very last one." Mollie smiles and focuses on me. "So, hero, any thoughts on your senior quote?"

"I think I know what I'm going to write. I'd planned something else, but then some girl gave me a black eye and I had to rethink things," I say.

"What were you going to write?"

"I don't know. Something like 'Do not let your fire go out. Spark by irreplaceable spark. In the hopeless swamps of the not quite, the not yet, and the not at all, do not let the hero in your soul perish. The world you desire can be won. It is real, it is possible, and it is yours.'"

She looks at me, dumbfounded. "Whoa, Carly. That's beautiful."

I smile widely. "Moving stuff, right? I learned it from *One Tree Hill*."

"I can't believe you," Mollie says, shaking her head. "So what did you change it to?"

"Nope. Not telling."

"You do know you turn that slip in to me, right? And I type it into a computer?" Mollie says, eyes twinkling.

"Oh. I didn't think this through."

"That's Carly for you. She got all the looks and only some of the brains," Annie jumps in.

Mollie laughs. "I can see that."

"Wow, thanks," I gripe.

"Alright, I'm going to get yelled at if I hold up the line," Mollie says. "I'll take your papers. Here are your smocks. You can go to the photographers now. I'll see you around, yeah?"

"Yes, absolutely, for sure," I ramble awkwardly, until Annie pulls me away.

"If you ever get a date with this girl, it'll be a miracle."

A stone settles in my stomach. This is all happening so fast. Too fast. I have the makings of a crush, that much I think is obvious, but god forbid the world should find out. I don't want people to know because then there are all these expectations and weights on my shoulders. Not to mention, this could all end the same way it did with Emma. No, no, no. I can't want this.

"I don't know if that's what I want," I reply.

She stares at me like I've got a leg growing out of my

head. "Two days ago, you literally said you had a crush on her. I'm going to assume you suffered minimal brain damage from your black eye incident because that's the most absurd thing you've ever said. That includes the time you tried to convince me you had a genuine crush on Zac Efron."

We get separated to take our photos, and the woman taking mine looks at my black eye and asks if I'm sure I want to take this photo today. She seems genuinely shocked when I say yes. I put on the stupid smock and take a seat in front of the camera. My eyes wander to Mollie Fae and I smile instantly. So much for wanting to squash the crush.

The photographer takes the picture and I hand over my fake dress smock thing. She points to the computer behind her and says I can see a preview of the photo with my quote directly underneath. I'm quite pleased with the outcome. This is how my classmates are going to remember me forever:

Carly Allen
"You should see the other guy."

6

We're Going to Be Friends
by The White Stripes

By Wednesday, my eye has pretty much returned to normal. On the one hand, I'm happy about that because I was starting to get irritated by everyone constantly asking about it. On the other hand, I haven't seen Mollie Fae since picture day. Yes, I said I didn't want to encourage this crush, but on the other other hand, daydreaming makes tutoring class go by faster.

At the end of my junior year, one of my freshman teachers, Ms. Bennett, approached me about becoming a tutor. At first I was super taken aback because she knew better than anyone how much I'd struggled through AP bio and geometry. She assured me that the amount of actual scholastic tutoring was minimal and that I'd be more of a role model. Which seemed more up my alley. That, and it would basically be a free period. As the lazy senior I anticipated being, it sounded great to me.

All I do is make sure the freshmen are filling out their

agendas and doing their homework. Sometimes I'll impart my senior knowledge and give dating advice. The fact that these kids are dating as freshmen blows my mind. When I was a freshman, I could barely speak to cute girls, let alone figure out if they were gay or not. It was the school year after The Summer of Stella Carraway, but I was still a little shy and overwhelmed. Plus, I exclusively wore sweatshirts and ill-fitting jeans, so I doubt I was turning any heads. Oh, and that was the year my acne was out of control. I could've had a very successful career as a before model for skincare ads. Is it just me or are kids nowadays skipping their awkward early teen years? I'll get off my soapbox now.

Anyway, things changed and I've somehow become the type of person who's considered a role model. Proof that miracles happen every day. The tutor gig's been sweet, though. The kids like me and think I'm funny, and since I'm a very open, out, proud narcissist, that means I like them too.

"Carly," Ms. Bennett says when I walk through the door. "I'm glad you're here early. I need to talk to you."

"Yeah, what's up, Ms. B?" We've become as close as students and teachers can be. We don't hang out in public, but she steals me snacks from the teachers' lounge.

"What do you know about Claire?"

"Claire Glover? The girl in this class?" I ask, and Ms. Bennett nods. "Not really anything. She doesn't talk much."

"That's what I'm worried about," Ms. Bennett says.

"She's not doing well?" I ask, sitting on top of one of the desks.

She shakes her head. "We're worried she might not pass biology, which would make her have to repeat ninth grade."

"Oh, that's…bad," I say. Sometimes I hate talking to teachers because I have to censor myself. When I do, my vocabulary drops to that of a five-year-old.

"I was hoping you'd focus your energy on her for the rest of the year," Ms. Bennett says. "I made a new seating chart and I put you in an empty seat next to her."

"Okay, so you just want me to make sure she's doing her homework?"

"Yeah, and be her friend if she'll let you. Just try to get on her good side and make sure she's doing her homework correctly. Maybe you can help her after school with extra practice tests if you're up to it."

I shrug. "That sounds fine. No one deserves to have to repeat freshman year."

She laughs. "I like that attitude."

The first few kids come through the door and Ms. Bennett puts the new seating chart up on the projector. I find my name and take a seat.

Claire is the last one to walk into the classroom as the final bell rings. She isn't fazed one bit about it and barely acknowledges anyone at her new cluster of desks.

"Okay, class, go ahead and pass your agendas to the tutor at your table. They'll look them over while we get started," Ms. Bennett says.

I arrange the agendas so Claire's is the last one I'll look at. The other kids at the table have caught on at this point in the school year. Or they've mastered how to fake their agendas well enough to make me think they're doing okay. Whatever. I have no way of knowing for sure, but if they're putting that much effort into lying, good for them. Good enough for me.

Claire's is a disaster. She hasn't written a single assignment for a month. Why has no other tutor in class caught this? Who the hell was doing her agenda checks? No wonder Ms. Bennett thinks Claire isn't getting anything out of this program. Idiots aren't doing their job right.

I pass the agendas back to the kids and listen as Ms. Bennett continues her lecture on some new note taking method. Thank goodness she doesn't ask me to uphold all these skills in my life. I lost my agenda on the first day of school and my notebooks are filled with half-assed song lyrics and little drops of incoherent writing sprinkled around. There's a note in my economics notebook that says "demand." What inspired me to write "demand" randomly in a margin? Was I worried I would forget one of the few things I knew about economics before the school year started? Which brings me back to the overarching question;

why am I considered a role model?

The bell rings and everyone rushes toward the door. I grab my books and go after Claire.

"Hey, Claire! Wait up!" I say, jogging past her classmates. She makes no acknowledgment of my request. "Hey, so I'm Carly. Tutor in the class we were just in."

She remains silent.

"Okay, cool. So, can I ask why your agenda's empty?"

"I have nothing to put in there," she says curtly.

"She speaks!"

"Your Hawaiian dad shirt is tacky," Claire says, then pulls a faux shocked expression. "She speaks again."

"Harsh, kid," I say.

"Don't kid me," she says. "And stop following me."

"Take the teen angst down a couple notches. Your all-black wardrobe already conveys your disdain for the world." Probably not something I should say to a person I'm supposed to be tutoring, but whatever.

"Harsh, kid," she says, mocking me.

"Listen, I just want to know why you aren't writing in your agenda."

"Because it's a waste of time."

"That might be true, but how do you remember your homework?"

She shrugs. "Not worried about it."

I laugh. "Oh, I'd be worried about it. Do you want to

repeat ninth grade? Is that part of your rebellious teen angst five-year plan?"

She stops dead in the middle of the hallway. "I'm failing?"

I raise an eyebrow. How do you not know you're failing? "You're on the fast track to being the new Steve Underwood. Everyone loves a fifth-year senior."

"Shit."

"Yeah, so Ms. Bennett put me in charge of your academic career. We're gonna get you to pass, okay?"

"I'm going to fail," she says.

"Hey, pep up! I'm not going to let you fail."

"I don't pep up."

"Okay, well pep down then. I don't know. The point is, we're going to be spending a lot of time together."

She pulls a face. "I think I'd rather flunk out."

I cross my arms and stare at her. Claire huffs, exasperated. "Okay, fine, but don't wear Hawaiian dad shirts anymore. They make my eyes hurt."

"You're not really in a place to negotiate, or to insult me for that matter."

She groans loudly.

"Love that plucky, positive attitude," I say, clapping my hands together. "Now start keeping track of homework in your agenda. We'll talk later about some after-school study sessions."

"Study sessions?" she asks.

I start walking away from her. "You know it. I'll even wear my favorite Hawaiian shirt, just for you," I say, throwing in a wink for good measure.

"Oh my god."

7

Friday I'm in Love
by The Cure

As soon as I walk into the cafeteria, I see Annie wildly waving her arms. I give her a weird look and continue to the lunch line to get a soda, but then she starts yelling my name. Causing a damn scene. She's jumping up and down frantically now, so I give up on soda and head over to her.

"You yelled?"

"Hi, Carly. You know Todd? Remember him? From the party last weekend? That Todd. Remember him?" she asks, a mile a minute.

"Chill, Annie. Yes, I'm familiar with Todd," I say, dropping my backpack onto the seat.

"He'shavinglunchwithus."

"What?"

She takes a breath. "He's having lunch with us."

"Cool. Why is this a big deal?" I ask.

"Because I haven't talked to him sober," she says. "What if I'm boring?"

I laugh. "Annie, you had half a Mike's Hard. That's moderately tipsy at best."

"That's more alcohol than what's in my system right now," Annie says.

"Want me to go get you some rubbing alcohol from the science wing?" I ask, and she scowls. "You're gonna be fine. If things get weird I'll just tell that story about the time my grandparents smuggled an entire lamb carcass across three state lines and cooked it on a spit in my front yard."

"That sounds like a crazy story, Carly," Todd says, taking a seat at the table.

"Why, thank you, Todd," I say, looking at Annie, who's moderately terrified. I point to his copy of *The Scarlet Letter*. "You're in our English class, right?"

He nods as he opens his tin lunchbox with Wonder Woman on it. "Yeah, but I usually sit in the back."

"That's crazy. You should sit with us. There's a spot next to Annie. Isn't that right, Annie?" I ask, elbowing her.

She sputters. "Yeah, there totally is."

Todd beams. "Is it cool if I sit there tomorrow?"

Annie nods, a dumbstruck look on her face.

"Cool. That's decided. I'm gonna go get a soda. Anyone want anything?" I ask, standing up.

"I'm okay," Todd says.

"Annie?" I ignore her angry, pleading stare. "No? Good, I'll be back."

I walk over to the lunch line and see Claire sitting alone at a table. Poor kid. No matter how rebellious she acts, I doubt she really wants to sit alone at lunch. Once I pay for my drink, I take a seat across from Claire.

"Hey," I say.

She shakes her head. "No, there's no way we're studying during lunch."

"I'm not here to study. I was wondering if you'd like to sit at my table instead of alone in the corner by the trash can," I say.

Claire looks over to see Todd and Annie surrounded by some of the art kids we're friends with. "I think I'll pass."

"Oh, come on," I say. "I'll give you my Gushers."

"No one packs Gushers for lunch anymore. Are you five?"

"Only at heart," I say. "Now, let's goooo." I tug on her arm.

"Fine," she says begrudgingly.

We walk over to Todd and Annie, who've done a total 180 and are chatting like they've known each other since forever.

"Sorry to interrupt, kids," I interrupt, taking a seat. "This is Claire. We're in tutor class together."

"I'm failing bio," Claire says dramatically as she takes a seat.

"Hi, Failing Bio, I'm Todd," Todd says, holding his

hand out.

"Uh-uh. I did not come here for dad jokes," Claire says, standing up.

"Calm down," I say, pulling her back down. "A+ joke, Todd."

"Matches your dad on vacation shirt," Claire says, and I laugh.

"You're funny. Who knew?" I say dryly.

"I'm Annie. It's nice to meet you," Annie says. Claire smiles weakly.

"I think this is the beginning of a beautiful friendship," Todd comments.

"That's from a movie, right?" Annie asks. "I know it is. It's on the tip of my tongue."

"*Casablanca*," Claire says, and we all stare at her. She shrugs. "What? I have a grandmother."

"We're learning all kinds of things about you today," I say.

"Hey, Carly!" someone calls brightly behind me.

I turn around and see Mollie Fae holding a brown paper lunch bag in one hand and her school books in the other. I know it's the twenty-first century and she should probably know better than to use a brown paper bag for lunch every day, but I will go on record as saying that she looks really pretty as she's slowly killing the environment.

I clear my throat and only moderately stumble over my

words. "Oh, hey, Mollie. How're you?"

"Pretty good. You?" she says, walking closer.

"Good, yeah, good. How about you?" Claire snorts next to me.

Mollie laughs. "Well, since we last spoke, I'd say I got a little better. So, I'll go with very good."

"Sorry. Sorry, that was lame."

"No worries." I can't help but smile. She puts her hand on my shoulder and gives it a squeeze. "See you around?"

"For sure," I say in a whisper there's no way she heard. I yell after her. "For sure."

Mollie turns around, grinning, and gives me a wave. There are kids at every table around us staring at me because I guess I yelled quite loudly. Whatever. Sue me for being nervous.

"So," Claire observes, breaking my focus on Mollie walking away. "What was that about?"

"I have no clue what you mean," I answer, tossing the Gushers pack at her.

"That was weird," Claire says, opening the Gushers. "You're weird."

"I'll take those Gushers back," I say, trying to grab them, but Claire pulls them out of my reach.

"No one else thought that was weird?" Claire asks.

Annie laughs. "It was a little weird, Carly."

"Come on, Annie. You're supposed to be the one who

sugar coats it for me."

"Not much to sugar coat. You were awkward as hell," Claire says.

"It could've gone worse," Todd interjects.

"Thank you, Todd. Would you like to be my new best friend? I have a sudden vacancy," I say, glaring at Annie.

"I think it went fine," Annie comments.

"You trying to bang that girl?" Claire asks.

"I feel like you're not supposed to talk to your tutor that way."

Claire shrugs. "Don't care. That girl's hot. Good luck."

"Thank you?"

"Dunno what she sees in you," Claire says.

"Alright, alright. Get your insults out now." Why did I agree to tutor this girl?

"Does she like girls?" Todd asks.

"No clue," I reply with a mouthful of sandwich.

"How do you find out?" Claire asks.

"Ask her her favorite Tegan and Sara song."

"Who?" Claire asks.

"Exactly," I shoot back.

Todd and Annie get wrapped up in their own little world again, so Claire and I talk about the kids in our tutor class. It turns out that even though she's talked to very few of them, she's got a lot of opinions. She hates this kid named Jimmy because she used to sit next to him and he would chew on his pencil and eat the eraser. We're debating if the human stomach can break down rubber when the bell rings. I drink the rest of my soda as we walk out of the cafeteria.

"So when does this actual tutoring start?" Claire wants to know.

"Sooner's better than later. We've got a lot of work ahead of us."

"So the day before the final?" she asks.

"That eager to start?" I joke.

"No, but like, I don't know," she says. "I don't want to fail."

"I told you, I'm not going to let you fail."

Claire glances over at me. "I've got to go visit my grandma after school today. Tomorrow?"

I shake my head. "Can't do tomorrow. I have to work."

8

Night
by Bruce Springsteen

Like most other high school kids, I have a job. Mine is more for bulking up my resume than supporting my family, unless you consider my unhealthy obsession with online shopping to be a family problem. But, unlike most high school kids, I work in a record store. Spin Me, Baby is a Baltimore institution that's been here since John Waters ran the city. The guy who owns it, Scott, picked me out as his next prodigy. One day I was looking at a Beach Boys album when he walked over to me and said I was hired. I told him I hadn't applied for a job, but he just said "No one applies" in the weirdest, most cryptic old dude way. I told him I was fifteen, so I legally couldn't even work with him if I wanted to, but he scoffed and said he'd hire me the day I turned sixteen. Sure enough, on my 16th birthday, a card came in the mail from Scott offering me a job. I still have no clue how the hell he knew when my birthday was and I'm 80% sure I'm in a weird record store cult now, but I love it.

I love record stores. Most of the records in my personal collection are used ones. Yeah, read that sentence again and try not to roll your eyes at how nerdy I am. But I like used records, used books, even used clothes sometimes. They've got stories. Like the used copy of *Born to Run* I found. Who knows the life it had before it got to me? Let's go on a hypothetical time-traveling road trip to prove my point.

Somebody in 1975 (no, not the band) bought this album. That was 41 years ago. Maybe it was purchased as a gift or maybe someone woke up early to be first in line to buy it for themselves. Maybe it's moved across the country over and over again. Maybe the owner(s) spent hours dissecting the lyrics and maybe they hate Bruce Springsteen and it sat on their shelf for decades. There's no way to know what kind of life it led before it got to me, but it could've been someone's favorite album and now it's my favorite album.

I can tell you about the day I bought it, though. It was the summer before freshman year. The summer I affectionately call The Summer of Stella Carraway. Stella Carraway was my first kiss and my first real crush. We kissed a whole summer away under the stars of the elementary school playground. It was mulchy, giggly, and soft. We always met between dinner and family TV time. I remember waiting for her in the muggy night air under the jungle gym dome.

Ahem. Sorry about that minor detour.

Anyway, I bring up Stella Carraway because she was the one who took me to Spin Me, Baby for the very first time. Her mom spent summers touring with Journey selling merch for them. She's basically Penny Lane from *Almost Famous*. When she became a mom, she just passed all that music down to her daughter. It's how Stella and I became friends. We were the only kids in middle school who'd heard of The Beach Boys, Cheap Trick, and Fleetwood Mac. It might as well have been destiny.

One afternoon, Stella took me to Spin Me, Baby and I've gone back almost every day since. We were flipping through albums and I was somewhere in the As looking for ABBA because life's too short to hate ABBA. All of a sudden, there was a blurry record in my face. It took a second for my eyes to focus, but when they did, I saw it was a used copy of *Born to Run*. My favorite album. The one Bruce Springsteen album that was missing from my collection. That album was released in 1975 and now it had magically appeared in my life. When I think about the immensity of the world and the billions of paths it could have taken to get here, I get a headache.

That's time travel, folks.

"Carly Allen!" Scott yells from his booth. He's conservatively ninety-seven years old and if he doesn't shout, he can't hear himself.

Scott is my boss and the owner. I genuinely have no clue what his last name is. He's just this ancient man who loves music. He spends every single day here and I've never heard him mention any sort of significant other in his life. At least not a long-term, permanent one. He's become this weird fatherly figure to me. I mean, I already have a weird, hippie fatherly figure in my life who is my actual father, but I'll take all the weirdos I can.

"What's up?" I ask, lifting a box of newly donated records onto the counter for him to appraise. "These were dropped off a little bit ago."

"Ohhhhh," he exclaims, hugging the box. "I've got a good feeling about this box."

Scott skips giddily into the back booth that's crammed to the brim with records. I probably won't see him for the rest of the day, so I turn my attention back to the store.

We mostly have three types of customers here. There are the people who are a little younger than Scott who grew up with records but gave them all away once CDs and cassettes came out. Now they're back to buy all the records they gave away in the first place. Most of these people are just happy to talk about how they saw Joan Jett when she was still in the Runaways or how they slept with Mick Jagger. I like those people. But then there's that group of old people who bring up a stack of records to the register and say things like "Bet you've never heard of any of these singers" and they don't even have obscure albums. They're buying the Journey album that has *Don't Stop Believin'* on it. Those people piss me off.

And then there are the annoying hipsters who look around for hours without ever buying anything. They wander through the store and then come to the desk to complain that we don't have some dumb band they saw perform once at four a.m. in an abandoned glue factory with four other people. Sometimes I like to put on One Direction so they leave faster. One guy had the audacity to come up to me and talk about how I "lacked integrity" because I was playing "mainstream pop bullshit" at an indie record store. It was *Made in the A.M.*, which is probably their least mainstream album. I responded by putting on *Up All Night* which, for all you non-One Direction connoisseurs out there, is their most mainstream bubble gum pop album. I have zero tolerance for music snobs. I do realize that working at a record store automatically makes me a music snob, but I stand by what I said.

I like this job a lot. I get to sit back and just talk about music. Other kids are coming home smelling of McDonald's burger grease and I get to come home smelling like dusty old records. Nothing against McDonald's, but I love old records in the same way people love the smell of old books. Plus, I could never work at McDonald's because I have the wrong-shaped head for a visor and because the guilt I would accrue from lying about the ice cream machine being broken would keep me up at night.

The bad part about this job is that it's pretty solitary, which means I have a lot of unwanted time to think about my life and my feelings. After the events of the weekend (i.e., me re-meeting a very pretty girl), I haven't been able to think of much else. I'm a big believer in fate and destiny and all that nonsense because I watched *One Tree Hill* and *The O.C.* in my formative years. Those shows gave me unrealistic expectations of how romance is supposed to go. And '80s music. That is the most quixotic shit I've ever heard and I can't get enough.

I like to think of myself as a Seth Cohen type. Hopeless, artistic dreamer. Someone who would write a kick-ass comic book for the girl she loves. He's what I aspire to be. I like those shows, though, because the plot is insane and even though someone's long-lost, presumed dead sister comes back during sweeps week, you know Seth and Summer are going to make it. Same thing with teen movies like *She's All That*, *Bring It On*, *Clueless*, all of 'em. Except I'll argue that Torrance and Missy belonged together in *Bring It On* and it's nothing short of a travesty that Torrance ends up with Missy's *brother*. Her brother! Other than that and Stacey Dash's recent wild support of Donald Trump, things turn out how they're supposed to.

Do you know my favorite part of those teen movies?

It's when you get that shot of the main character sprinting down a hallway or through an airport to get to the one they love. Hopping over subway turnstiles, through TSA security, pushing, shoving. Sure of the world. Surer than their own name.

I love that. That unparalleled confidence in their feelings. I'm confident. I'm at home as the center of attention, but the two aren't the same. Give me a sold-out stadium of 55,000 and that's nothing compared to having trust in myself. Clearly. Why should I believe in myself? At one point in recent years, I thought orange corduroy pants were cool. Obviously, I can't be trusted.

I would kill for that confidence, though. Having utter clarity. It's like the part in *One Tree Hill* where Nathan takes a game-winning free throw, but only watches his girlfriend, Haley, the whole time. Of course, he makes the shot and the team wins. When I saw that I was like, so that's what true love is. In retrospect, I might've been a little misguided. Nathan being able to make that shot without looking at the basket probably says more about his basketball skills than the caliber of his love, but it got me good. Never in my life have I done anything with total assurance like that.

9

You're My Best Friend
by Queen

It's Sunday afternoon. Annie and I are flipping through the channels and the only thing we can agree on is *Tiny Homes*. I love *Tiny Homes*, but I hate the people. Listen, you're on a show called *Tiny Homes* and you're genuinely shocked when the Realtor shows you a home that is tiny? What did you expect? A tiny mansion? No. You get a tiny home with a weird composting toilet, a fold-down ladder to your loft bedroom, and no cabinet space in the kitchen. Accept it and move on.

"So how'd your first official date with Todd go?" I ask.

Annie grins instantly. A wide, all-her-teeth-visible, enormous grin.

"That good, huh?"

She nods. "Carly, he's such a sweetheart! And he actually dressed up like it was a date."

"Marry that boy."

My number one pet peeve with all you straight people,

aside from homophobia, is the weird phenomenon of how inadequately boys dress for dates. I don't even date boys and it really annoys me. So often you see a couple out for dinner or at the movies and the girl's dressed to the nines. Not full evening gown formal, but she's clearly made an attempt to look nice. And yes, I recognize that a woman can dress nicely for herself and not for a man, so put the pitchforks away. It's just that a date is supposed to be different. All full of nerves and excited breathlessness. You dress to impress. So you've got all these girls looking nice for boys who are wearing khakis and t-shirts with holes in the armpits. Moral of the story, boys, please dress better.

"What did he wear?" I ask, grabbing the pretzels from her lap.

"He wore black jeans and a pastel short sleeve button-up."

"Did he steal that from my closet?"

She laughs. "He actually mentioned something along those lines because I was talking about you, like I always do. He said you were in a few classes together and he thinks you're pretty funny. Plus he thinks you dress nicely."

"He's ass kissing for my blessing and I 100% give it to him for saying I dress nicely. Why can't girls compliment me like that?"

"I'm pretty sure you've got a girl who wants to give you compliments like that."

I wave her off. "We're not talking about me. Tell me more about Todd. Did you two go see a movie?"

"We'll come back to you," she says. "We saw *Hail, Caesar!* I think it's called that. I didn't fully get it because Todd went on and on about how it was a love letter to old Hollywood. I just wish Channing Tatum had taken his shirt off."

"Glad you appreciate fine cinema for the talent and creativity it showcases."

"Todd really cares about movies in the same way you care about music. It's just like I'm dating the straight, movie-loving dude version of you. He cares about cinematic integrity. I care about hot men and the amount of time they spend shirtless." Annie pushes her hair back. "But I had a lot of fun. He made the perfect number of jokes under his breath during the movie. We walked around Hunt Valley after and we even sat and held hands by the fire pit."

"Did he kiss you?"

"I haven't gotten there yet."

I groan dramatically and slide off the couch. "You're killing me."

"I'm almost there," Annie says, pulling me back up. "So we're driving back and he stops in front of my house, turns off the car and says, 'I know this might be cliché, but can I walk you to your door?'"

"I'm vomiting."

She bumps my shoulder. "We get to the door and I'm so nervous because I feel like he could kiss me and the last boy I kissed was Bobby Radcliffe. Remember him? Utter disaster. Anyway, I'm nervous, he's nervous, and my parents could very well be inches away on the other side of the door. Then he says, 'I think this is the best date I've ever been on. Do you think it'd be okay if I kissed you?' And words would not form in my brain, so I just nodded and then we made out for a solid ten minutes against the door. Until we heard Bear barking and I had to push him away. He kissed me one last time because neither of us wanted to deal with the impending parental onslaught. Then he ran to his car, shouting that he'd call me tomorrow."

"Annie, that's the sweetest thing I've ever heard. I think I just developed the bad kind of diabetes from that. Come here," I say, pulling her into a hug. "I'm just so stupidly happy for you, kiddo."

She kisses my cheek, real sloppy like she knows I hate. "I think I could really like this guy."

"I would hope so. He sounds fantastic. Does he have a gay sister I can date?"

Annie pulls away. "No, but I heard Mollie doesn't play totally straight and narrow."

"Who told you that?" I ask, trying desperately to keep a

sudden surge of enthusiasm under some semblance of control.

"Steve Underwood. Well, kind of in a convoluted way. He was talking nonsense about how she rejected him at a party recently, and therefore she must be gay because who wouldn't want to go out with a god like him. A+ reasoning on his part. Then Veronica's like, get your head out of your ass, Steve, no one would date you. To which Steve flips her off. Then little Lucas, you know, the cute, quiet boy with the lisp. He says he thought he saw her holding hands with some Delaney girl at a jazz concert a couple months ago."

"Of course Lucas goes to jazz concerts. That doesn't mean anything concrete about Mollie, though," I say, hoping Annie doesn't notice the change in my demeanor.

"Exactly what I thought. So I texted Morgan from Delaney who I took driver's ed with and asked if she knew anything about a girl from her school dating our very own Mollie Fae. She said she did and that the girl's name was Taylor. She didn't even ask me why I wanted to know."

"That speaks wonders about your friendship," I mumble.

Annie glares. "I stalked Taylor on Facebook, and sure enough, quite a few damning photos. Lots of profile pictures of her and Mollie together in a coupley way. According to Morgan, though, they broke up a little bit ago."

"Huh."

"'Huh?' That's all you have to say? After all the information I just dropped on you?"

"It's just a lot to process," I say, turning back to the TV.

"No, no, no," Annie says, turning off the TV. "It's not a lot to process. This pretty girl, who you like quite a lot I might add, is being handed to you on a gold, gay platter and you've suddenly lost interest."

"I haven't lost interest, I've just got a lot to think about now, Annie. Turn *Tiny Homes* back on."

"Not until you tell me why you're acting so weird. She's gay or some part of that alphabet soup of letters and she was flirting with you. What else do you need?"

"Nothing, I guess," I say, letting my head fall back against the couch.

I feel Annie shift next to me. "I'm just going to chalk this up to you being on your period or Mercury being in retrograde or something." I smile a little at that. "You know if something's up you can always talk to me, right?"

"Of course. I was with you when you were in diapers. You're stuck with me until we have to be in diapers all over again."

She ruffles my hair. "I love you."

I feel a tear roll down my cheek because yeah, Annie's right. My period's right around the corner and I'm always an emotional wild card in the days leading up to it. One time, I cried at aquamarine. No, not the movie, just the color because it was a really nice color.

"Love you too."

"And you will tell no one I was in diapers in kindergarten," Annie says, flipping on the TV again.

I laugh. "I'm saving it for my best woman speech at your wedding."

****

Annie left about an hour ago and dinner with the fam has transitioned into movie night. It's my dad's turn to choose and he picked that terrible Zac Efron DJ movie that I don't even need to see to know it's terrible. My dad really loves my mom, but I think he'd leave her for Zac Efron in an instant. I gave the movie a good twenty minutes before I lost interest and grabbed my laptop from the other room under the guise of doing homework. I hope I can find someone who won't give up on me as fast as I gave up on this movie. Geez, are those my only standards? They keep getting lower and lower. Maybe someday I'll even date a Republican.

HA. That'll never happen.

I open a Word document because I have a paper on *The Scarlet Letter* due soon. I don't even remember what the paper's supposed to be about. You know, if people really want to know why literacy drops off in young adults, it's because they make us read these horrible books. No one in the history of the world has ever uttered the words "My favorite book is *The Scarlet Letter*." Literally no one. *Romeo and Juliet?* Probably. *To Kill a Mockingbird?* For sure. But *The Scarlet Letter* is pure garbage. Take total offense, Nathaniel Hawthorne. It should come as no surprise that I end up stalking Mollie's ex on Facebook instead.

Let's say I stumbled across her page by total accident. I found Annie's friend who she mentioned earlier and then just happened to find Taylor when I searched through her friends. What a coincidence. In retrospect, I should've just looked through Mollie's friend list, but where's the fun in that? And would you look at that? Taylor's profile is 100% open to the public. I love technologically inept people. They make my life so much easier.

She's cute. I'm adult enough to admit that. Nowhere near as grotesque as I'd been picturing her/wanting her to be. She's got a short haircut, but like a tacky Justin Bieber one. OG JBiebs with the swoosh hair. Full disclosure, I did have that haircut in middle school, but no one knows better in middle school. Tragic haircut aside, she's not awful.

Before I know it, I'm clicking through photos. There's one of her and Mollie where I think Mollie was kissing her on the cheek. Another one of Mollie asleep on a couch with a puppy on her chest with the caption "no new friends." I begrudgingly respect that aptly used Drake lyric.

It goes on like that for a few months. I'm pretty sure I can pinpoint that they started dating in early October and broke up in early January. I've moved past judging this girl and now I'm starting to feel jealous. I want to have pictures with Mollie like that. Which is stupid and dumb because what's the point? Graduation's in three and a half months and then I'm out of this town like a rocket.

"What's got you looking like that, Carly?" my dad asks.

"Oh, uh, nothing," I say, trying to close all the incriminating tabs. "Just *The Scarlet Letter.*"

"It's about a girl," my mom says, not even looking up from the quilt she's sewing.

"Mom!"

"You've got a girl on your mind, kiddo? Should I pause the movie?" my dad asks, sitting up a little straighter.

"You should just turn it off."

"What's her name?" my mom asks, still sewing.

"Hey, there's nobody. Not since Emma."

"Yeah, whatever happened to that girl? You were so happy," my dad says, looking over at me.

I stare at him incredulously. "Seriously? Dad, she cheated on me months ago."

"Oh, right," he says, snapping his fingers. "So you two broke up, then?"

I close my laptop. "I think I'm just going to finish this

70

in my room."

"You'll miss the end of the movie!" I hear my dad yell as I reach the top of the stairs.

"One of his friends is going to die and he bangs the girl," I shout back down. I Googled the synopsis five minutes after the movie started.

I throw myself onto my bed and decide I haven't wallowed in enough self-pity yet, so I open Taylor's Facebook page again. Their stupid faces are there, smiling over and over and over again. In a hallway, at a football game, in a car, in a field of snow. Did they pay a photographer to follow them around? It's a little excessive. I'm being a little excessive. She's just some girl I met once freshman year who I hadn't spoken to again until last week. I need to get a grip.

10

Best Song Ever
by One Direction

Claire and I spend the tutoring period going over practice quizzes. I don't think this girl has ever paid even a second of attention in a single biology class. Can't say I blame her, though. I hated biology. It was next to impossible and I begged my mom to let me drop from AP to the regular class. She took that as a personal insult to her ability as a biologist. Her exact words were "I will not have a daughter who doesn't get an A in AP biology."

Bits and pieces of my biology knowledge come back to me as I look over Claire's notes. She's still not really putting in the effort she needs to, and I have no idea how to change that. Shockingly, I don't have much knowledge of ways to encourage people to apply themselves. I have never been applied in my life. I mentioned this to Ms. Bennett the other day and she said she'd think about what to do.

The bell rings and Ms. Bennett says, "Carly and Claire, I'd like to see you before you leave."

Claire swears under her breath as we pack up our stuff.

"What's up?" I ask as we get to the front of the classroom. Claire hangs behind me.

"Claire, Carly has expressed some concern about your progress," Ms. Bennett begins. I can feel Claire glaring behind me.

"Okay," Claire says.

"I think it would be best if you spent some time with Carly outside of school, Claire. It will help you see that hard work pays off in all aspects of life."

"Would you want that?" I ask, looking over at Claire, who's shaking her head no.

Ms. Bennett ignores that. "Let her hang out with your friends. Show her some positive role models."

"Like go to a movie?" I ask. Claire looks down at her shoes, scuffing the floor.

"You could do that. I was thinking of something more interactive," Ms. Bennett says.

I have no clue what Ms. Bennett wants from me. "Laser tag?"

"Or you could take her along to your band practice," Ms. Bennett says.

Claire's head jerks our way. "What do you mean, band practice?"

****

73

"So, um, Claire, this is the band. Band, this is Claire. I'm her tutor," I say from the doorway of Bryan's garage.

"Why'd you bring her here?" Bryan asks from where he's hunched over the piano, tuning his bass.

"Great warm welcome," I say, pushing Claire into the garage and pulling the door closed behind me. "She's here because Ms. Bennett thinks Claire needs more positive role models in her life and she believes we qualify."

Bryan laughs. "Yeah, okay. Only Heather's a good role model."

Heather shrugs. "We're happy you're here, Claire."

"See?" Bryan exclaims.

"Great!" I say, clapping my hands together. "Now someone has acted like a decent human being. Let's get to know everyone, shall we? The asshole on the bass is Bryan. He's only in the band because he has a garage. Heather plays drums. Matt and Mark are twins and play guitar. And yours truly is the lead singer."

"Are you any good?" Claire asks, taking a seat on an amp.

"Of course." Me.

"Sometimes." The twins.

"Hell to the fucking no." Bryan.

"I guess." Heather.

"Wow, what rave reviews," Claire scoffs.

"At the end of the day, it's kind of hard to screw up

One Direction," Bryan says, shrugging.

"Wait. One Direction? Are you a One Direction cover band?"

I sigh. "Yes."

"I can't believe Ms. Bennett wants me to take life advice from a One Direction cover band," Claire says, laughing openly. "How are you popular, Carly?"

I shrug. "Ladies love One Direction."

"I can't believe this. Will you guys play at my cousin's birthday party?" Claire asks.

"We'd have to check," one of the twins says. "It's mitzvah season, so we're pretty booked."

Look, I know it's terrible and totally unacceptable at this point, but I can't tell the twins apart. We've been in this band for two years and I still have no clue which one's Matt and which one's Mark. After two years, though, I can't really ask who's who.

Claire starts laughing again. "Oh my god, stop. I'm tearing up. I'm so happy Ms. Bennett made me come here."

"Yeah, yeah," I say, plugging the cable into the mic.

"Can you guys play me something? Can I film this for your graduation slideshow?" Claire asks.

I roll my eyes. *"Best Song Ever?"* I ask the band.

"I will never agree with that name in relation to this song, but yeah. Why not?" Bryan sighs, taking a pick off the amp next to him.

When the song ends, I turn and look at Claire. "So, what'd you think?"

She's staring at me, her mouth open. "Why are you actually a good band?"

Bryan laughs. "We're jazz band dropouts."

"I wanted to hate it so badly. You shouldn't be good. I should be making fun of this!"

"So you think we're good?" I ask with a grin.

"No," she says, but there's no conviction there.

"I'll take it," I say, putting the mic back on the stand. "See? We're better than a ten-year-old's birthday parties!"

Bryan plays a bass riff. "So, what? You wanna take this party on the road?"

"I don't think our mom would let us," one of the twins says.

"Think slightly smaller," I suggest.

"Church barbecues?" a twin asks.

"Synagogue barbecues?" the other twin asks.

I shake my head. "Less religious."

"Cameron's End of Year Extravaganza?" Heather asks as she pushes her glasses up.

I smile like a movie star. "Cameron's End of Year Extravaganza."

"Don't you want to get drunk and make out with that girl you can't stop drooling over instead of playing music?" Claire asks.

"Not now," I wave her off.

"Realistically," Heather clears her throat, "no one is going to want to listen to a One Direction cover band for the whole party."

"I definitely don't," Bryan scoffs.

"That's fine. We'll play a few because that's what people know us for and everyone can dance to the super popular songs," I say. "But we could do other stuff. We'll learn the Top 40."

"Aren't you too pretentious for the Top 40?"

"I am, but come on!" I say, gaining momentum. "We could be good! Claire even sort of admitted it. That's the highest compliment we've ever gotten. Think about it. The party would be fun. We'd play for people our own age instead of crying kids. Don't you want to have just like a taste of minor success?"

"I think it could be fun," says one of the twins sheepishly.

"I mean, it is *almost* a real gig," Bryan says.

"I doubt I'd be invited otherwise," Heather says.

"Let's do it!" says the other twin.

It's a wonder we got this far with these levels of enthusiasm.

11

Can You Tell
by Ra Ra Riot

"When will any of this be at all useful in my life?" Claire groans.

"When you become a parent and have to help your kids with their bio homework," I say, looking over her practice test.

"What a wonderful thing to look forward to," Claire says. "I bet you want all that nonsense. Kids, picket fence, minivan."

"Mmmhmm," I hum. "Especially when you phrase it like that."

I finish grading her practice test and hand it back to her. "Not too bad. Solid C."

"Am I going to pass with a C?"

I hesitate. "I mean, technically, no. But you're getting there."

"So great, I'm still failing," Claire says, slumping down in her chair.

"Yeah." I try to be positive. "But you're failing slightly less now."

She glares at me. "You're shit at this tutor thing. Aren't you supposed to be encouraging me?"

"I am! I said it wasn't too bad. That's encouraging, right?"

She stares at me. "In what world is that encouraging?"

"I think you might need to put some extra work in at home," I say.

"Isn't that what got me here in the first place? Not doing things at home? You want to rely on that as the thing that will make me not fail?"

I sigh. "Could you at least try a little to do some homework?"

"I'll think about it," she says, looking out the library window. "Hey, isn't that the hot girl you embarrassed yourself in front of?"

I whip around in my chair and sure enough, there's Mollie Fae. She's looking at the flyers hanging on the window.

"I swear, Claire, do not wave her down," I say harshly.

"Too late," Claire says, waving to get Mollie's attention.

"Claire!" I shout, swatting at her arms.

"It's fine. She knows me from gym class," Claire says. "Oh, good, she's coming inside."

"I will murder you."

"Hey, Carly. Hey, Claire," Mollie says when she approaches our table. "What are you guys up to?"

"Studying," Claire says. "Carly's gonna help me pass ninth grade."

Mollie turns to look at me. "That's so nice of you."

I shrug. "I do what I can."

"Why're you here after school?" Claire asks.

"My mom was supposed to pick me up and take me to my brother's baseball game, but she forgot. So I don't have to go to a baseball game, but now I have no ride home."

"I could drive you," I say quickly.

"Oh, no, I don't want to interrupt your study time," Mollie says.

"I think we can wrap up a little early today." Claire starts packing things up.

"No, no," I say. "We still have like three more worksheets to do, but then I could drive both of you home."

"Oh, come on, Carly, haven't we worked hard enough?" Claire asks, pouting.

"Yeah, come on, Carly." Mollie starts pouting as well.

I look at the two of them for a minute and then give in. "Fine. But you're going to do them at home, yeah?" I pass Claire the worksheets.

I'm pretty sure Claire's quietly swearing at me as she stuffs the worksheets into her bag.

"It's the beat-up blue Jeep," I say as we walk out to the parking lot.

"Shotgun!" Claire yells and runs to the car.

"No way," I tell her. "You're the youngest, so you're in the back."

"I won fair and square," Claire says as I unlock the doors.

I look over at Mollie, who's opening the back door. "Sorry. She's a little intense."

Mollie just smiles. "Don't worry about it. She won fair and square."

I put the key in the ignition and silently pray it starts on the first try. The stereo kicks on as the car sputters to life and my Bruce Springsteen mix CD fills the car.

"What the hell!" Claire exclaims. "Who is this person? He sounds like he's dying."

She moves to change the song and I slap her hand. "You aren't changing it."

"Passenger picks the music. That's the rules."

"Yeah, well, driver makes the rules and that's a dumb rule," I say.

"He's a dumb singer," Claire grumbles.

"You're a dumb singer," I shoot back.

"Settle down, kids," Mollie says, putting a hand on each of our shoulders.

"Who even is this?" Claire asks.

"Bruce Springsteen."

"Who?" Claire and Mollie ask at the same time, their tones wildly different.

"Oh my god, like the cornerstone of American rock and roll. *Greetings from Asbury Park, Born to Run, Born in the U.S.A., Nebraska.* Nothing? He's my all-time favorite singer," I say. "But I'm going to change it because someone is being childish."

"Who?" Claire asks again.

I sigh. "I'm going to let you play your music because you're exhausting me."

"Wonderful," Claire says, pulling out her phone.

I catch Mollie's eye in the rear view mirror and swerve ever so slightly. She notices, and a sly grin crawls across her lips. It's such a cute, annoying grin. I just want to kiss it right off. I swerve again.

"You sure you have your license?" Claire asks, scrolling through her music.

"Just put something on," I say, switching the stereo over to the aux cord setting.

Rap music I've never heard before comes blaring through the speakers. The bass is turned up so high, it sounds like a nonsensical, garbled mess in my ancient speaker system. The entire car is shaking.

"And you called my music garbage?" I yell over the

noise.

"This is good stuff, right, Mollie?" Claire asks, turning around in her seat.

"I don't think Carly and I are the target audience for your music," Mollie shouts. My heart does a cartwheel when I hear her refer to the two of us as a we.

"What's that supposed to mean?" Claire asks, finally lowering the volume.

"I think Mollie and I like sad guys who play guitar and sing about girls who broke their heart," I say, looking at Mollie in the rear view mirror.

She nods. "Sounds about right."

"That sounds terrible," Claire says. "I'd rather die."

"Don't be so dramatic," I respond. "Now tell me where to turn."

"Left on York and then it's the road that has the pizza place," Claire says. "Wanna stop and let me get some pizza?"

"No."

"Maybe if you listened to less sad music, you'd stop being so lame." Claire slouches in her seat.

"What's that? You want me to be more lame? You want me to break out my corduroys and my pastel floral shirt for school tomorrow?"

Mollie giggles in the back seat as Claire groans.

"I think you'll damage your vocal chords if you keep

making noises like that," I say with a smile.

"Yeah, and I'll go blind from looking at your horrific fashion choices." Claire looks out the window. "It's that house on the left."

As I pull into the driveway, Claire unplugs her phone and gets out of the car. She gives us a small wave and turns to walk toward the house.

I roll down the window. "Want me to pick you up tomorrow for school so everyone can see you walk in with the cool kid in the pastel floral shirt and corduroys?"

Claire turns around and glares at me. She starts violently shaking her head no and I laugh and roll the window back up. I turn to look behind me and I'm met with Mollie Fae climbing over the center console. She drops into the passenger seat and flashes a brilliant smile.

"My turn to pick the music," she says, winking.

We spend the drive to Mollie's house singing loudly to the Spice Girls. I'm nervous to actually sing in front of her, so I pretend to be really bad and sing horribly off-key. It makes her laugh and laugh, doubled over, holding her stomach. After way too short a drive, we arrive at Mollie's house.

She goes to unbuckle her seatbelt and says, "Want to come inside for a little bit?"

12

You Make Loving Fun
by Fleetwood Mac

"And I thought I had a hippie New Age dad," I say, looking around her room.

Mollie has decorated her room with flags from countries around the world and a bi pride flag, which officially puts that question to bed. Speaking of beds, above hers is a massive old American flag that has a peace sign in place of the fifty stars. Beads hanging in front of her closet. Tie-dye shirts strewn on the floor. There's a corkboard hung over a desk covered in knick-knacks and books and pieces of scrap paper. The table that holds her record player is immaculate, as is the bookshelf that has the records. All the music is categorized by genre and then alphabetically, just like mine.

"I knew you'd go straight to the records," Mollie says as she takes off her jacket and hangs it in the closet.

I laugh. "I do work at Spin Me, Baby for a reason."

"Play something," she says and sits on the bed.

I don't think I'm breathing. Here I am, in this beautiful girl's bedroom and there she is, on her bed. I don't expect anything to happen. I didn't at least. But all of a sudden, it feels like something could and that terrifies me to my core.

"Close your eyes. It'll be a surprise."

I pick Fleetwood Mac's *Rumours* because, well, it's Fleetwood Mac. What else can I say? Perfect amount of casual listening music with the underlying romance of Stevie Nicks. Anyone could fall in love listening to the magic of Stevie Nicks' voice.

"Fleetwood Mac," Mollie says, eyes still squeezed closed as *Second Hand News* crackles on.

"You're right. Springsteen and One Direction are my go-tos, but your collection is a bit lacking," I say, awkwardly standing in the middle of the room.

She opens her eyes, blinking to adjust to the light. "I can't say I've seriously listened to either one." She pats a spot on the bed next to her. "Come sit."

I kick off my shoes and slowly climb onto the bed next to Mollie. We sit in silence as I continue to look at the things that make up her room. We're not sitting close enough that we're touching, but we're close enough that if I turn my head, she'd be the only thing in focus. Something about that proximity and Stevie Nicks' voice might just send me over the edge.

"What are you thinking about, Carly Allen?" Mollie

asks.

You, my brain screams.

"I was just trying to figure out where you keep your crystals," I say, chickening out. Guess there's not enough magic in Fleetwood Mac.

She laughs loudly. "I'm not *that* much of a hippie. My parents are. They've got that weird salt rock lamp thing in their room. I like the classics. Like tarot cards."

"Since when do tarot cards qualify as a classic?"

She shrugs. "To me they are. I've been using them since I was a little kid."

"Did you have tarot card school instead of Sunday school?"

Mollie laughs again and I feel the magic returning. "No, nothing like that. Just as a hobby. I'd use them when I couldn't make a decision about something."

"You let cards decide for you?" I ask.

"No," she says and pauses to think, running her hands through her hair. "It's like a way to see the situation more clearly. Based on the cards, maybe I'd see something different or get a different perspective. It sounds silly, I know. To me, it's like asking all your friends for their advice and then taking the average. Since we moved so much, I didn't have friends to poll and there are things you don't want to talk to your parents about."

"Okay, yeah," I say, finally looking over at her, only to

find that she's looking right at me. "That, uh, that really makes sense."

"Want me to read your tarot?" she asks softly, and I feel the world move further and further away as I look into her eyes.

They're a nice green. Light enough that I can see each of the itty bitty crystals that make up the iris. I've never been good with eyes. Staring into them for a long time weirds me out, so I avoid eye contact when I can. My mother thinks this is going to hinder my job search in the future. Let's return to The Summer of Stella Carraway to fully understand why I'm like this.

It was nearing the end of that most blissful summer. I was supposed to meet Stella at the playground as usual at around 6:30. Out of nowhere, hands covered my eyes and a voice asked me to guess who it was. I knew the feel of her fingers. They'd spent the summer touching my jaw and my hair, and my stomach on nights when we felt particularly adventurous. I said her name and she kissed the top of my head.

Stella sat in front of me now, her eyes squeezed shut, and asked me what color eyes she had. I laughed and said I had no clue. That was the absolute wrong answer to give to a fourteen-year-old girl. She stormed away and I cried alone on that playground until it was time to go home and watch *Survivor*.

I haven't seen Stella since. I think she transferred to a private school. This was the time when a lot of kids didn't have cell phones. That night still leaves a sick taste in my stomach. I should've remembered her eyes, but eyes don't usually stick out to me. Lips and hair and hands are the things I remember. I dated Emma for almost a year and I don't think I could make the right guess about the color of her eyes. But then there's Mollie. I get it now. I understand all the hype about people's eyes and the window to the soul and all that nonsense. I couldn't forget Mollie's eyes if I tried.

Eventually, my brain remembers she asked me a question.

"Uh, I've never had my tarot read," I stutter.

Mollie flashes a wide grin. "You're in luck," she says, and uses my thigh to push herself off the bed.

"I'm nervous. Should I be nervous?" I wonder aloud, wiping my palms on my pants.

"You'll be fine. I'm not going to put a hex on you or anything," Mollie says, rummaging through knick-knacks.

"Whew, that's good to hear," I say.

"Scooch." She shoves my leg.

I move to the foot of the bed and Mollie sits with her back against the headboard, legs crossed. She's fiddling with the deck for a while before she looks up and asks, "What do you want, Carly?"

"Huh?" That's all I can get out.

"What do you want to know? What questions does the heroic Carly Allen need answered?" She tucks her hair behind her ear.

"Oh," I laugh a little. "I don't know."

"Come on. No tests you're worried about? Friendship problems? Crushes you want to know if they like you back?"

"I'm not worried about that," I say, looking right at her.

She blushes. "You shouldn't be. You're quite the catch, from what I hear."

"You can only believe half of what you hear."

"Okay," she says, shifting. "So, you're fine romantically and socially. Oh, I know! Have you figured out college yet?"

"Definitely have not done that," I say. "Have you?"

"Stanford. Pre-law. I want to save the world." She smiles. "Cross spread it is."

And she's off. Do I understand a word she's saying or a thing she's doing? No. All I can pay attention to is the cadence of her voice and the way her fingers flip each card. She takes the last card and turns it over. The supposed outcome to my question.

"Oh, shit. That cannot be good," I say. The card has a dude hanging with a noose around his neck. The Hanged Man.

"Remember what I told you," Mollie says in a sing-song voice. "No card is bad."

"Tell that to the man who's hanging himself," I say. "Does this mean I'm going to die at college?"

"Carly, calm down," Mollie says, putting her hand on my knee. "All it means is that the only way to be in control or win is to just let go. Surrender. Something tells me that despite your chill demeanor, you actually need to be in control."

She's 10,000% right in every way. "I mean, I guess there's some truth in that."

"Mollie! Are you home?" A woman's voice comes through the hallway.

"I'm in my room!" Mollie yells back, then more softly. "That's my mom."

"I figured. That or the world's worst burglar," I say.

"Oh, I didn't know you had a little friend over," Mollie's mom says as she walks in. "And look at you. So cute."

I blush and Mollie groans. "Moooooom."

"What's your name? Since my daughter seems to have lost all the manners I taught her," Mollie's mom says, walking over to the bed.

"Carly. Carly Allen, ma'am."

"Well, aren't you the gentlewoman," she says as she ruffles my hair. Something about having short hair makes people think it's okay to touch it whenever they please. Like the strangers touching pregnant women's stomachs effect.

"Is Doggy back from the vet?" Mollie asks.

"Sure is. And a little shy because of the cone," Mollie's mom says. "Put on that album Doggy likes. Maybe that'll help."

"Okay," Mollie says and hops off the bed.

"And, Carly, you just give me a call if you need anything, alright?"

I nod as I hear the crackle of the needle on whatever record Mollie has picked out for her coned dog. The opening notes of *Stop! In the Name of Love* come through the speakers and there's frantic pitter patter down the hallway. A coned dog slides past the door on the first try.

"I can't believe you named your dog Doggy," I say.

"Yep. Doggy Ray Cyrus. You know, business in the front and a party in the back."

By that, she means Doggy Ray Cyrus only has two legs. In place of back legs is a set of pink glittered wheels that light up when Doggy picks up enough momentum. Between the cone and the wheels, this dog just exudes ridiculousness.

Mollie's singing along and Doggy Ray Cyrus is dancing around her feet. Really, just circling around her. Doggy tries to pop a wheelie, but the new weight of the cone throws off the balance.

I'm sitting on the bed, mystified by the scene in front of me. Mollie's hair is bouncing as she dances the twist for her bedazzled, disabled dog. That may sound like a strange vision, and it really is quite the scene, but all I can think about is how happy I am to be here.

"Dance with me," Mollie says excitedly.

I stand up and walk over to her. I hate dancing. I can't do it. I move like an awkward dad on vacation after one too many piña coladas. All shoulders, no hips. It's embarrassing and certainly not going to win anyone over. However, through trial and tribulation, I've learned that when a pretty girl asks you to dance, you dance. Inhibitions be damned.

13

Dancing in the Dark
by Bruce Springsteen

I'm on the floor and knee deep in dusty records when I hear the bell on the door chime. "Hey, welcome to Spin Me, Baby. If you need me, I'm behind the counter."

"Avoiding your customers, Carly Allen?" a voice above me asks.

I look up and there's Mollie Fae, leaning over the counter, hair falling over her eyes. My mouth and brain have a hard time getting started. "Oh, hey, Mollie. What're you doing here?" I ask, standing up and wiping the dust off my hands.

"Thought I'd stop by. Check out this Bruce Springsteen you can't stop talking about," she says, sliding off the counter.

I run my hand through my hair. "Yeah? You liked him?"

She shrugs. "We'll see. I want to give him a fair listen without Claire talking over him."

I laugh. "Follow me," I say, walking toward the records.

"I actually was looking for cassettes," she says, putting her hand on my arm.

"Wow, cassettes, really? People give me shit for collecting records and here you are," I laugh, "still collecting cassettes. You got a *Say Anything* boom box, too?"

She winks and takes her hand off my arm and I miss it instantly.

"Cassettes it is," I say, and start making my way over to the cassette section.

"So how'd you get this job? I thought the person who owned the place didn't like other people working here. I've never seen a help wanted sign."

"Scott saw me looking through the records about three years ago and was like 'I dig your groovy vibe, I'm going to hire you on your 16th birthday.'" I start flipping through the S section.

"What a dude," Mollie says, leaning over my arm to watch as the cassettes flick by. Her hair tickles my bicep and I shiver.

I clear my throat. "So, any Springsteen album in particular?"

"You choose."

"Well," I say, picking up a few albums, "we're having a buy two used cassettes, get one free sale."

"Oh, really?" she asks, skeptically.

"Yeah, it's a uh, a new promotion for, you know."

"Hmm?" She moves closer so we're shoulder to shoulder.

I look over at Mollie and I could kiss her right now. I've thought about it many times and here's this moment right in front of me. My mouth goes dry and my heart speeds up. There are centimeters between us. Centimeters that could disappear in a millisecond. But I can't move. There's that voice in the back of my head that's talking shit. Saying that if I didn't deserve a girl like Emma, why would a sweet, nice girl like Mollie waste a second of her time on me?

The bell above the door rings and I jump away from Mollie, blushing wildly. A long-haired hipster walks in and starts browsing the records. The weight of the moment dissipates.

I clear my throat. "So, uh, one of those is my favorite album of all time," I say, handing her the cassettes.

"Which one?" she asks, flipping them around and reading the track listings.

I shake my head and start walking back toward the cash register. "Not telling."

She pushes my shoulder with her own. "Not cool. I want to understand you on a spiritual level."

"You sound like Scott," I say, jerking my thumb to the

back booth where he's sitting. His eyes are closed and he's holding a record up to his nose, inhaling deeply.

"I'm serious," she says, putting the cassettes on the counter. I give her a look. "Okay, kind of serious. It's interesting to listen to people's favorite songs. Mixtapes used to do that."

"Ah, yes, the lost art of mixtapes," I say as I start scanning the cassettes.

"I make a mean mixtape. Been making them since I was a kid. Sick *Barney* and *Sesame Street* mixtapes to start. No one appreciates them anymore. To be fair, I listen to really sad music. Not everyone's cup of tea," Mollie says, rooting around in her tote bag for her wallet.

I take a dive off the highest dive in the world. "You should make one for me."

Her head jerks up. "You have a tape player?"

I gesture in front of me. "I work in a record store. Having outdated music devices is basically the only job requirement. I even have an eight track player."

"Well," she says, putting her credit card on the counter. "Play your cards right and maybe you'll get one."

My cheeks flush furiously. This really has to stop. "I'd like that," I say, putting the cassettes in a bag.

"Thank you," Mollie says, grabbing the bag and putting her wallet away.

I print out a little slip of receipt paper. "Text me when

you listen to the albums."

I can't even bring myself to look at her. My hands are shaking as I write my name and my ten stupid, stupid digits. The last four are worse than the rest. It doesn't matter. It's readable and hopefully somewhat endearing since it shows how nervous I am. I push the paper across the counter and finally meet Mollie's gaze. Her eyes are wide and her cheeks are a little pink. Have they been that pink this whole time?

She takes the paper and folds it so neatly, so softly. I see the pink on her cheeks spreading. She bites her lip as she folds my note again. "You will be the first one I text."

"Good," I say, letting myself get lost in her beautiful green eyes, the gold flecks dancing in the fluorescent lights. "Good."

"Yeah, good."

"What's so good?" Scott yells, coming out of the booth.

"Hey, Scott. Just, uh, some music shop talk."

"Hmm, what'd you get?" Scott asks loudly in Mollie's ear, taking the bag out of her hand.

"Go ahead and look," Mollie says.

"Oh-ho-ho. Springsteen. You've been hanging out with this little working class dreamer over here, haven't you?" Scott asks, elbowing her in the side.

"Just a little," I say.

"A little," Mollie agrees.

Scott gives Mollie back her bag. "Good choice."

"Well, I should probably head out. Leave you to your customer service," Mollie says. "I'll see you tomorrow."

"Tomorrow," I nod.

When she's out the door, Scott turns to me and asks, "You getting jiggy with that girl?"

"What? What are you – no, Scott, geez," I say, and I see the hipster in the store stare in our direction.

"Whoa, whoa," Scott says, holding up his hands. "Slow down. So, y'all aren't getting jiggy?"

I sigh. "No. I don't think she even knows I maybe possibly would want to, you know, get jiggy with her."

"Oh, trust me. That girl knows. She knows. You've got a neon sign blinking over that gorgeous head of yours," he says, ruffling my hair.

"Scott!" I squirm, pushing his hands away. "You think so?"

"Kid, I'm going to play you a song to answer that question for certain."

He paces around the store for a little while, flipping through records. He finds what he's looking for wedged between a display shelf and the back wall. Dust clouds follow him as he walks back to me and the record player.

"This," he says, holding up a nondescript album cover. "This is going to answer every single one of your questions about that girl. Then it'll answer questions you didn't even know you had."

I raise an eyebrow, extraordinarily unconvinced. "Let's hear it."

The needle catches and it's the worst thing I've ever heard in my entire life. It's some kind of experimental '60s psychedelic nonsense. Scott's screeching along to the melody, eyes closed, swaying to what I'm assuming is the beat. It's pretty hard to tell. It just sounds like a pterodactyl shrieking and wailing with synth nonsense in the background. The government should torture people with this album. I can't handle it anymore, so I jerk the needle off the record.

Scott opens his eyes abruptly. "Major party foul, dude."

"Sorry," I say. "Just too many answers at once, you know? Kind of made my head feel like it was going to...." I mime my brain exploding.

He nods. "It'll do that to you. You lasted longer than most people on their first listen," he says, putting the record back in its sleeve. "I knew you were special."

"And you," I say. "You sure are something."

He's too busy shoving the album back into its space between the shelf and the back wall to notice my response. I take out the ABBA greatest hits album I keep behind the counter and give it a spin. Scott dances his way back to his booth and I'm alone again, replaying every single detail of Mollie's visit.

14

The Way You Do the Things You Do
by The Temptations

"What is this movie about again?" Annie asks as we walk into the theater.

"Lesbians," I say.

"So my chances of shirtless man scenes are next to nothing?" Annie asks.

I nod as I test out a couple of seats, looking for the one that's in the perfect middle of the screen.

Annie sinks into a random chair. "We're watching *Magic Mike* when we get home."

"Can we watch the second one? That's the better one," I say, deciding on the seat next to Annie.

"You're the only person in the world who likes that one better," Annie says, opening her purse and pulling out our snacks.

I take a box of Junior Mints from her. "Thanks. I only like that one because of Amber Heard. Plot wise, the first one's leagues better."

Annie laughs. "I love that you're talking about plot and *Magic Mike*. It's like talking about, well, I don't know. I can't think of two things that clash as much as *Magic Mike* and plot."

"Plaid and argyle," I offer, chewing.

The movie hasn't started yet, so I pull out my phone to see if Mollie's texted me. The rational part of me doesn't expect her to because she left the store only a few hours ago and four albums is a lot to listen to. However, the irrational, love-drunk part of my brain is running in overdrive and incapable of processing any other thought.

"Are you going to keep checking your phone all night?" Annie asks.

"Hmm? No. I'll put it away when the previews start," I say.

Annie looks at me funny. "Who are you waiting for a text from?"

I shake my head. "No one."

"You hate texting. You barely text me," Annie says.

"How do you know I'm not waiting for an email?"

"No one under the age of thirty is waiting for an email," Annie says.

"People email. That's a normal thing," I say.

"I'm sitting next to you, so who else could you be texting?" She thinks about it for a little, then smacks my shoulder. "You gave Mollie your number!"

I shush her. "Yes, okay. Calm down please. People are staring."

"Carly Allen," Annie says, smiling.

"Annie Montgomery," I say, irritated.

"I can't believe you gave her your number," Annie says.

"Yeah, so she could text me her thoughts on the Bruce Springsteen albums she bought. Nothing else."

Annie scoffs. "Carly, I'm going to be completely honest. No one likes Bruce Springsteen. I'm your best friend and I can't listen to more than one of his songs."

I check my phone again; nothing. I groan. "Modern dating is the worst."

"You sound like my grandfather," Annie says, then puts on an old man voice. "When I was your age, I met your grandma for some G-rated dancing and soda pop down at the sock hop before my weekly meeting of Racists R Us," she says, then uses her normal voice. "You need to chill."

"I'd for sure go to a sock hop," I say.

"Maybe you should've been a '50s greaser," Annie says, opening her candy.

"The '50s just seem so idyllic. Everyone dressing up nice and going to the Friday night party. You find a pretty girl, ask her to dance, and give her your letterman. Boom. The end."

"Maybe Mollie's afraid of your unrealistic expectations and incorrect knowledge of historical times," Annie says.

"Not funny," I say, putting my phone away.

"Speaking of historical times," Annie says, suddenly nervous. "I got into college."

I turn to her. "You did? Where?"

"Pitt. Nursing," she says shyly.

"Annie, that's incredible!" I pull her into a hug. "That's the one you wanted, right?"

She nods into my shoulder and pulls away. "Yeah, and I got an almost full scholarship."

"That's really real. Like you're going to your dream school!"

"Yeah," Annie says. "It doesn't feel real."

"I can imagine," I say.

"Have you figured out where you're going yet?" Annie asks.

"Nope, nope, nope. Don't want to think about it."

"You haven't mentioned anything about college. Did you even apply?"

"Of course," I say.

"Okay, well, did you get in?" she asks.

I wave her off. "Don't worry about it."

Annie tries to ask me another question, but I shush her as the lights in the theater go down. I relax in my chair, kicking my feet up onto the seat in front of me. I could go on and on about how rude I find it when someone comes into an almost entirely empty theater and chooses the chair with my feet on it, but I feel my phone buzz.

"Shit," I whisper.

"What's wrong?" Annie asks.

"My phone buzzed. It could be her," I say.

"Carly Allen, you will not take your phone out. Do you know how many times I've listened to you complain about people who use their phones in movie theaters?" Annie whispers back.

"I know, but it's just the trailers. If I don't look it's going to eat me alive for the entire movie and I won't be able to enjoy it."

I pull my phone out and unlock it.

> Your Discover Card Statement is now available. Minimum payment due: $35.00
> Text STOP to quit.

"You've got to be kidding me," I groan.

Annie takes the phone from me and reads the text. She laughs through every single preview while I sit here suffering. To make matters worse, some asshole sits in the seat my feet are on. Is there no justice in this harsh, cruel world?

It's a good movie. The lesbians live and it's implied they end up happily together, which is in stark contrast to most lesbian movies and TV shows. I try explaining all that to Annie and the repercussions of this positive narrative, but she thought it was a snooze fest.

"I mean, it was good, but not write-home-about-it good," Annie says as we walk out of the theater.

"But *Magic Mike* is worthy of owning?" I laugh.

"I told you," Annie says, also laughing. "No one is watching it for the plot. The same way no one is reading *Playboy* for the articles. The same way you're not watching all of Anna Kendrick's movies for their cinematic importance."

"Hey!" I say, "*Rocket Science* is really good."

"And so is *Magic Mike*."

"I'm so done with you." I pull my phone out of my pocket.

I like to think of myself as a generally grounded person. Enough of a dreamer to believe wholeheartedly in love, but with my feet on the ground. The perfect 50-50 creation of my hippie father and biologist mother. Talk about genetics and Mendel and mixing genes. I've got enough of a hippie brain to fall in love 90 times a day and enough of an analytical brain to be able to rationalize.

Yet here I am, grinning like a damn fool over this girl's first text.

> Hey it's Mollie!! How're you??

There are many things about this five-word text that have me reeling.

"Why are you smiling like an idiot?" Annie asks.

"She texted me," I say, holding up the phone for her to see.

Annie studies it for a minute then says, smiling, "Huh. And they say romance is dead."

15

Crimson and Clover
by Joan Jett & the Blackhearts

I'm lying in bed at three a.m., thinking and thinking and thinking about school and life and what happens after death and what went on in people's minds before we created language and just every ridiculous thing my brain can come up with. Nothing good happens after two a.m., right? That's certainly true when it comes to my brain.

The little glow-in-the-dark stars that my parents and I hung when I was in elementary school are still on my bedroom ceiling. It was when I was learning about outer space. They're in the pattern of the summer sky because I liked how central the Hercules constellation is. Back in the Disney days of my youth, *Hercules* was my movie. Heroes, mythological villains, and a kick-ass love story? Sign me up. A good portion of my understanding of love is based on that movie. You've got this girl who literally trades the entire package (you know, life, liberty, and the pursuit of happiness) for love, and when it's all said and done, the guy just shits on her. Probably the harshest blow in any film that's ever been written. You think *Sophie's Choice* was rough? No, no. Ten-year-old me was devastated when Megara's boyfriend ran off with some other girl while Megara wasted away in Hades' Underworld.

Of course, *true* true love wins in the end. You can say whatever you want about Hercules and how he's supposed to be the hero in this story, but that's not right. Sure, he's the son of Zeus and Athena, an accomplished monster slayer with rippling pectorals, the real Grecian deal. But Meg was the hero for me. The girl who chose others and the prospect of love over her own well-being on two separate occasions, despite the first instance ending so badly. I never understood how she could do that. And yeah, I get that it's an animated movie and things always end happily ever after in them. Whatever. That movie still makes me cry.

I want that certainty in my life. I know a few things at this present moment for sure, 100% certain. 1. *Hercules* is the greatest movie on the planet. 2. I think I could possibly, maybe like, *like* Mollie Fae. 3. I want to be more sure of more things. Like take this Mollie Fae thing, for example. There's the distinct possibility that Mollie Fae could be lying in bed just like me, thinking about me in the way that my mind is endlessly circling around her. And there's also the distinct possibility I'm alone in this, but I'm holding out hope. That's the stupid thing, though. I'm holding out hope for what? That we'll make out a couple times? Is that what I'm rooting for in this scenario because I'm too chickenshit to even entertain the thought of anything of more consequence? I know there's more out there and I know there are countless ends to this story and I know that so much of it could be altered by me, so why am I in neutral? Why is the only outcome I can fathom one that doesn't amount to anything of substance?

The phone on my stomach lights up and I see the name Mollie Fae all bright and pretty and I instantly forget the internal debate that's raging in my brain. I unlock my phone.

> You still up? Finally listening to that Sprigsteen man of yours. Want to hear my thoughts?

My heart rate picks up and my head says be cool, but I am not, nor will I ever be cool.

> I'm going to ignore the misspelling of Bruce's name and assume it was an autocorrect fiasco, BUT TELL ME EVERYTHING

I instantly throw my phone to the end of the bed because that'll for sure handle this situation and tone down my now compounding anxiety. It's fine. It's so chill. I mean, she must want to talk to me because it's three a.m. and lesbihonest, Bruce Springsteen is not interesting enough that she couldn't wait until tomorrow. Maybe she texted back. I mean, it wasn't the worst possible text I've ever sent. I'm sure it could have been so, so much worse. At least it didn't say, "Bruce Springsteen? More like, Bruce I-wanna-make-out-with-you-Steen." That was my first draft, so what I sent is a step up, but come on, it was still garbage.

I'm just going to look at my phone. It's fine if she didn't reply, that'd be okay. It wouldn't be a big deal because we're just friends and she already texted me once unprompted, so that counts for something, right? It's fine. My stomach is in knots that are knotted in other knots that are all tied together. But it'll be fine either way. Okay. I'm just going to get this over with.

Absolutely nothing. Just my solar system background staring back at me, mocking me. My love life is as empty as space is vast. I unlock the phone and open our texting thread because I hate myself and I'm a masochist. Not even the three little typing dots. Just blank. My idiotic, not-chill-at-all response is going to sit there. Might as well tattoo it on my head because this is inescapable. OH MY GOD. I want to punch Apple and Steve Jobs in the face. What did I do to deserve this?

At this rate, I should just set my phone on fire and pray that I can block this out of my brain entirely. Never again will I attempt to connect with someone. This is just plain ridiculous. My life is sent into turmoil because I'm overreacting to a one-sentence text message. The worst part is that I can't stop checking my damn phone. It's been like fifteen minutes and yet every single time a tiny glint of light catches the screen, my heart picks up a little and I think, "Oh, I'll forgive you for not responding in a timely manner. It's not like you have better things to do because it's three a.m.," but it's still nothing. I should just give up and become a nun.

And then she texts me back.

I definitely see why you like him. He's just like you embodied in a song. Is that creepy? Sorry if that's creepy, but I could totally see you in that album cover with the American flag and the handkerchief in the back pocket. You know the one? Of course you know the one, that's dumb. But I think I could like some of his songs. Definitely not The River like what even was that, but Born to Run. That's the one, right?

OMG.

I know I'm not the type to say OMG, and I've certainly never said it before, but I think there's no other word (Is OMG a word? Whatever. That's a whole separate issue.) in the English language to sum up my feelings at this present moment. I feel like I just won the Nobel Peace Prize and like I'm weightless on the moon. Hope springs eternal. Like so, so, so eternal. Remember how rotten my life was mere minutes ago? Yeah, forgot that already. I'm brighter than the sun. I'm on top of the world. I'm every dumb cliché you've ever read and rolled your eyes at. I am that in this moment.

> Hahaha yeah Born to Run is my favorite. I could write essays about the structure of that album and how it should only be listened to on vinyl but I don't wanna scare you away

There. That was chill, right? Casual, calm, collected. Her response is instant.

> If The River didn't scare me away, nothing will

I laugh openly. This girl's listened to Bruce Springsteen for a day, max, and she's already making jokes. I click my phone off, let it sit on my chest, and run a hand through my hair. I've built up a wall of sorts. I don't think I planned it or wanted it, but I think sometime around Emma leaving, a construction crew moved into my chest and started quietly building. Like Donald Trump's wall between the U.S. and Mexico, except the people living in my heart aren't illegal immigrants and getting kicked out. All the people who were already there (like my mom, dad, grandpa, grandma, Annie), they all get to stay. But this stupid wall means that no one new has been admitted. No one like Mollie Fae.

It's a damn shame too. I feel my heart growing little by little every time I'm around her, and especially now. I feel like my heart could burst, but there's something there that refuses to budge. Like when you're trying to start a fire and you've got matches and a ton of sticks, but they're all wet and there's no hope of it catching. It's here. The potential is real and it's simultaneously within my grasp and so far beyond my reach.

I don't know if I can blame all of this on Emma. It's college and how I feel like I'm letting my mom down if I don't become a biologist but I'm not even sure I want to be a biologist and the general self-doubt that comes with being a teenager. It's how the first girl I really truly allowed myself to go out on a limb for saw me as dispensable. It's all the things I kept telling myself didn't bother me because they're arbitrary, and the rational part of my brain knows that, but it's not enough anymore. It's piling up and I can't see a way out of it.

Here's the thing. I love who I am. I really do. I just feel so inadequate. Not good enough in school, not good enough in a relationship, just plain not good enough, and it's like a paralysis thing. I can see these feelings are wrong and misguided, but overcoming them is like what I imagine Everest looks like from base camp. I'm so sure of so many things, but I've never in my life been sure of myself.

16

To Leave Something Behind
by Sean Rowe

School passes uneventfully. Claire and I spend our lunch period studying for a quiz she has coming up. The kid's actually working really hard to get herself out of this hole. We don't talk much about her personal life and she seems fine with that. I think she's just happy someone's worried about her. I can't blame her. Isn't that what we all want? If you come from a stable background, you kind of take it for granted because you never question whether you have the home team rooting for you.

I take the long way home after school. It's spring, so the snowball places have opened their doors and that's where I'm going. A snowball's basically shaved ice with a bunch of sugary sweet flavoring added. A Maryland snowball isn't the cheap kind you get at state fairs. Our ice is shaved thinner and there's melted marshmallow dolloped on top. There was a snowball place on my walk home from elementary school and in the spring, once a week, I'd take some change out of my dad's change bowl so I could buy a snowball on the way home. I'm sure he knew because he'd open the door and my blue tongue would instantly give me away.

Elementary school's still in session, so I'm the only one there. I order the same thing I've ordered since I was five. A small Superman shaved ice. Who decided the Superman flavor would be blueberry? Like what a weird correlation. I take a seat outside on the bench and watch the cars drive by. My family moved here when I was four, so I really don't know anywhere else. I like this place. As much as I'm excited to leave it, I'm also petrified I won't get the chance.

When I finish my snowball, I realize it's almost time for dinner. I make my way home, park, and check the mail. There's a small letter addressed to me from Johns Hopkins and some magazines. I take the letter and shove it deep into my backpack before opening the door and heading into the kitchen.

"Any mail from schools today, kiddo?" my dad asks, standing by the stove.

"Oh, Dad! What on earth are you cooking?" I exclaim, holding my shirt over my nose.

"Lard. Bought a couple cans of it," he says proudly, holding the pan out to me.

"Lard? How can we possibly be having lard for dinner?" I ask.

117

"You want to try some?" my dad asks, holding out a spoonful.

"No! Why is it liquid?" I move away from his waving spoon. "Mom, we're not eating whatever this is going to turn into, right?"

"Of course we are, honey," she says, pressing a kiss to my forehead. Then she lowers her voice. "There's pizza in the back of the fridge."

"Thank goodness."

"You still haven't heard anything from colleges, though?" my mom asks.

I grab an apple and shake my head. "Nuh-uh."

"That seems very strange. I was talking to Annie's mom and she's already received quite a few letters. Maybe you should call the admissions offices."

"No, Mom, I'm sure they're super busy," I say quickly. "I mean, think of all the kids applying to colleges. They've got to be bogged down, and I feel like calling them is a sure-fire way to get them to reject me."

"I'm sure the universe is working some cosmic magic," my dad says, licking the lard spoon.

I stare at him, grossed out. "Yeah, cosmic lard magic I'm sure is working in my favor."

"I still think you should write to them or give them a call," my mom says.

"Okay, okay. I'll talk to some kids from school and see

if they've heard anything," I say, grabbing my backpack. "I'm going to get started on homework. Let me know when the lard becomes something moderately edible."

I walk upstairs to my room and pull a shoebox out from under my bed. It's where I've been hiding college rejection letters from my parents. There are at least nine now, from all over the country. NYU, UCLA, Pitt, Penn, UVA, Vanderbilt, USC, Boston College, and Johns Hopkins, as of today. I know what you're thinking. Those schools are all top of the line and I shouldn't be upset. Their admission percentage is less than the probability of me getting pregnant and that's very low. I'm not worried about them, though. I applied to those schools as a biology major to make my mom happy. She's implied that she wants me to follow in her scientific footsteps. I don't think I want that.

There's a letter in here from Oberlin, my dream school. Yeah, Oberlin, as in Ohio. Ridiculous, right? Who in their right mind would want to go to Ohio? Well, I do. I really, really do because I want to write. Nobody knows that. Annie has an inkling, but my parents certainly have no clue. I never took writing in school because the thought of having other people read and critique what I wrote sounded absolutely awful.

It's stupid, I know it is. The rational part of my brain is aware of how I should be letting people read my work and critique it. That's the only way I'll get better, but I can't. The double-edged sword is that I want to know if I'm good at this. I love it. I love it so much and it feels so simple. Just me and my words in notebooks tucked inside pillowcases. It's like Schrödinger's writing career. I can go on pretending I'm at least mediocre because being bad might just end me. I have no desire to open the box.

The letter from Oberlin is small and I remember how my heart fell out of my body when I took it out of the mailbox. In the college world, size matters. The thought of reading a rejection letter from my Plan A (literally my only real plan) was potentially too fundamentally life altering, so I jammed the letter into the shoebox of rejection and ignored it for two days. I finally cracked at like two a.m. one day and read the letter.

They accepted me, scholarship and all. The letter said they liked me so much they chose me as a prospect for advance acceptance to their creative writing school. All I had to do was send them a sample of my work and they'd give me the verdict in two to three weeks.

I tried and tried to write something I deemed to be profound. Something that would make them say, "Look here. We've got the next Alice Walker on our hands." Since getting that letter, I haven't been able to write anything. All the old stuff I've written looks like elementary, nonsensical jumbles that belong in the garbage.

All of my baseline emotions come from writing. Everything I know, I've worked through with a pen and a piece of paper. It's like coming home and finding a little puppy running toward me. That's what writing is to me. Coming home. And that's why I can't write something for Oberlin. I can't have some person in some room in Ohio of all places who's been reading other kids' stories all day tell me if I'm good. What if they say I'm not? Thanks for playing, find a new dream. No, I can't do that. I can't put the love of my life in the hands of a person from *Ohio*. I'd rather just never find out.

17

We Are the Champions
by Queen

Leave it to Annie and Todd to find the only mini golf course in town. It's a hokey monster mini golf place with black lights and animatronic monsters that have already made me jump more times than I'm willing to admit. However, I'm still kicking both of their asses at this game.

"Ohhh, look at that! One under par," I say, doing the Tiger Woods celebratory fist pump.

Todd's staring at me with his club behind his head. "Are you on the school golf team?"

"Nope," I say, shaking my head. "Grandfather was a golfer. Plus I'm a lesbian, so double whammy."

"I'm not sure you being gay affects your golf game," Annie says, taking a few practice putts.

"Pure science. Look at our golf team," I say, balancing on the rocks they tell you not to walk on. "Total lesbians. All of them."

"I thought Carrie was dating a boy on the guys' golf

team," Todd says.

I shrug. "Okay, there's one outlier."

"I'm chalking your score up to dumb luck," Annie says.

"I'm insulted. Name the time and place and we'll rematch."

"Fine," Annie says, finally putting. "You, me, Todd, and Mollie. Next Friday."

"Nice shot!" Todd says as Annie's ball makes it in.

"Why did I have a feeling that's where this conversation was going to go?" I pull out the scorecard. "What was that? Three over par?"

"Two over," Todd says, fishing out the balls and walking to the next hole.

"I was there when you got that text from her and you were ecstatic," Annie says. "I'm supposed to believe you've suddenly moved on?"

"No," I sigh. "I'm just taking things slow."

"How slow?" Annie asks. "Slower than glacial?"

"I mean, at the rate the ice caps are melting, glacial isn't that slow," I say.

"You know school ends soon, right?" Todd adds as he takes his first putt.

"Yes, thank you for your concern, but it's fine," I say. "If it happens, it happens. If not, it's fine."

Annie shakes her head. "You can't live like that."

"What about destiny?" I say, jumping onto the broken

windmill. "*Moulin Rouge*, right? Windmill. Get it? Isn't that movie all about destiny? You love that movie, Annie, and I love you despite that."

"You like *Moulin Rouge*?" Todd asks. "I love *Moulin Rouge*."

"You two are so perfect together," I say.

"Carly, you can't just say destiny and then not do anything," Annie says. "You have to put yourself out there."

"Then what's destiny supposed to do?" I ask, taking my turn. "I thought destiny was supposed to do all the heavy lifting."

We all watch as the ball goes through the windmill and a monster jerkily pops out of the top. I jump a little despite how slowly it moves. I'm not the best when it comes to things that jump.

"Is that a hole in one?" I ask, walking around the windmill. "Yes! Suck on that, windmill monster!"

"How are you doing this?" Todd asks. "My ball's in the hedge over there."

"You're ignoring this whole Mollie situation, though," Annie says.

"I don't know what else there is to say," I reply. "I don't know if I really like her."

"Bullshit."

And it is bullshit. I can barely admit it to myself in my

own head, so there's no way on the face of this planet I could possibly admit it out loud. If I say it, it becomes real. It becomes a thing I have to deal with and be concerned with. If it's only in my head, I can continue to act however I want. If I say it, it holds weight and that scares me.

"Listen, it's not a big deal," I say.

"Yes it is. This is a total 180 from where you started," Annie says.

"Not a total 180," I say.

"You had the biggest grin on your face the night of Cameron's party. Remember that?"

"Yeah, so what? I was smiling. Lots of things make me smile. That doesn't mean I want to date everything that makes me smile."

"You're being absurd," Annie says. "It was different. I know it. You know it. Todd even probably knows it. Why are you pretending it's nothing?"

"I don't want to give this Mollie thing more credit than it's worth," I say.

"But you're not even trying to give it any credit! Don't you see?" Annie exclaims.

"Because maybe there's nothing to try! This is just an endless cycle of going back and forth."

"Maybe we shouldn't talk about this anymore," Todd says quietly.

"Yeah, maybe we shouldn't," I respond, frustrated.

Annie sighs. "I'm sorry, Carly. I didn't mean to push you, but you're my best friend. I'm rooting for you."

"Yeah, yeah, you love me," I say, letting myself cool off.

"Come here," Annie says and pulls me into a hug.

"Group hug!" Todd yells and piggybacks onto the hug.

"I'm suffocating!" I say. "Suffocating! Somebody!"

"So melodramatic." Annie untangles herself from the hug. "But I feel like you're not telling me everything about Mollie."

I groan. "I thought we weren't talking about this anymore."

"And we aren't," Annie says, picking up her dropped club. "But in case this whole situation has made you forget you have a best friend who cares about you and will listen to your problems, this is me reminding you."

I smile. "Same goes for you. Heard you're dating a schmuck."

"Hey! Don't bring me into this," Todd says.

"Don't worry, I like you, Todd," I say. He smiles so big I wonder if his face might just split in two. "What I like most is how much I'm kicking both of your asses."

Annie shakes her head. "Carly Allen's back, ladies and gentlemen."

I take a dramatic bow. "Thank you, thank you. No, really, thank you. I'm here all night."

18

I'm on Fire
by Bruce Springsteen

I don't know why I'm here. Okay, that was dramatic. I know why I'm here. There's a party tonight. Big meteor shower at like two a.m. What do art kids love more than pot? Space. Naturally, they're throwing a massive party.

Annie and Todd bailed after mini golf, so I was totally ready to go solo to this shindig. Annie and Todd's words have been echoing in my brain and they've taken over. They're why I'm here, idling in front of Mollie Fae's house. I feel like an idiot. I should've texted her instead of randomly showing up in front of her house. Well, I'm here now, so I might as well woman up and invite her.

I toss a rock at Mollie's window and it hits the brick just below it. They make this look so easy in the movies. Is my hand eye coordination that abysmal? I go through ten rocks and finally hit the bottom corner of the window. I toss another one that's more of a direct hit. A small light comes on in the room and Mollie's head peeks out.

"Carly Allen," she says quietly, and I can't contain my giddiness. I feel like I've never heard my name properly pronounced until now.

"Mollie Fae. Fancy meeting you here at this time of night," I say, putting my hands in my pockets.

She laughs. "What are you doing here? Isn't your mom a super light sleeper? How'd you sneak out?"

"Out the window like any other honest American teenager. There's a meteor party tonight and I remembered how desperate to party with the art kids you were, so I made a pit stop."

"You're inviting me to a party?"

"Sure am."

"When does it start?"

I pull out my phone. "An hour ago."

A shoe comes flying out the window at me. "What the hell, Carly!"

"What? You almost just killed me!" I yell, as quietly as I can.

"You can't invite a girl to a party that started an hour ago!"

"Why not? This is a chill evening. Just throw on some jeans and a shirt. No biggie," I say.

I dodge another shoe that gets flung from the window.

"Listen," I say, "you don't have to come if it's going to cause you this much stress."

She huffs, then brushes her hair back. "You know, you're lucky I like you."

I smile stupidly. "I am."

Mollie stares at me for a while longer, a grin spreading across her face. Slowly, surely it builds until it's just the two of us staring at each other like a couple of fools at midnight on a school night.

I break the magic. "So, are you getting dressed or are we just going to stare at each other 'til morning? Because I'm fine with either outcome."

"Fine, fine. Give me five minutes." She disappears back into her room.

Exactly five minutes later, Mollie's climbing out the window like she's done it a hundred times. She makes it to the lower overhang before dropping lightly to the ground.

"That was so stealthy. In a dress, nonetheless."

She beams. "Pass me those shoes will you?"

Mollie grabs my shoulder to brace herself and pulls her sandals on. Then we're off, her hand in mine, tugging us toward the car.

****

The two of us are driving and I'd be lying if I tried to say I'm not nervous. That's, honestly, probably a gross understatement. I wipe my palms on my pants quickly at a stoplight, hoping the friction will dry them faster. There are millions of butterflies fluttering at the edges of my stomach. It's not like we haven't spent any time alone together. We've talked before, but it feels different when it's past midnight on a school night. I see Mollie playing with the hem of her dress. Folding, wrapping, creasing. I want to reach over and grab her nervous hand, but two shaking hands don't make a steady one.

I've never been shy like this around girls. With Emma it was always loud, loud, loud. It was like going a million miles an hour with the windows down. The roar of the wind was our norm. We fought and argued and laughed so loudly. There was no truly quiet moment. I was always quick to plug the silence with a story. She made me afraid of what could come out of the silence. You know, talking about the future, nitpicking the way I eat pizza, whatever. There's a whole lot of silence when it comes to Mollie.

I hear the opening harmonica of Ryan Adams' *Come Pick Me Up* come over the radio. This man is a genius. A twenty-first century Bruce Springsteen. And even though it's a song about how shitty first love is, I could fall in love a thousand times over while listening to this song. I look at Mollie again. She's staring out the window and I feel like this is a scene right out of a movie. The perfect midnight driving song with a pretty girl in the passenger seat and the open road empty and sprawling up ahead. It's miraculous, this moment. It's not loud and that's throwing me for a loop, but I feel it heavy with importance. Smothering even. I think I'm going to remember Mollie and this car and the broken blinking stoplights until the end. Maybe she'll still be there when I can't remember it anymore and maybe that's absurd. Maybe this moment is irrelevant and I won't even remember it next month. Maybe I'm doing some nervous fast-forwarding tic, trying to read the last page of my own story.

There's a park not too far from our homes called Oregon Ridge. We're not in Oregon and there's not a super-pronounced ridge, so the name's a total mystery. The park itself closes at sundown, but there's a whole picnic playground area that stays open. Well, not technically open, but no one polices it. It's before the big fence and padlocked gate. If an art kid throws a party, you'd better believe it's happening at not-so-Oregon Ridge.

When we get there, the party's already in full swing. Teenagers are all over the playground, drunk idiots trying to make the swings go all the way over the top. On the picnic tables are some Sam's Club chips and snacks and copious amounts of alcohol.

"Carly!" a boy says, running up to us as we reach the picnic pavilion.

"Hey!" I say. "What's up?"

He slurs. "You gotta sing tonight. I heard you sing at my brother's Jewish man party. You were so good."

I awkwardly laugh. "My band isn't here."

He smacks his forehead. "Good call, Carly. I'll catch you later then!"

He gives me one of those weird bro half-hugs before running in the direction of the kids smoking pot by the fence.

"Good friend of yours?" Mollie asks.

"I'll be honest with you," I say, looking over at her. "I have no clue who that was."

"You're joking. He really knew you. He knew your name and your band and everything."

"I'm just so bad with faces and names," I say, grabbing a water bottle out of a cooler. I offer to get one for Mollie, but she declines.

"You remembered mine after three years," she says.

I choke on the water. "Uh, that's different."

"How?" she asks in this faux innocent way that makes me believe she knows exactly why it's different.

"I don't know," I say flatly.

I do know. Everyone knows. Aliens who watch earth as primetime reality TV know. Heaven forbid I say it out loud, though.

"I'll just consider myself lucky," she says, tucking her hair behind her ears.

You're wrong, Mollie. I'm the luckiest person on this planet.

"So, is this the whole party?" she asks, gesturing at the groups of kids.

"Not yet," I say. "Joe will show up with his DJ kit soon and there'll be a dance party. You can see the stoners are already higher than a kite by the fence. One time they got so high they thought this was the forest from *The Blair Witch Project*, and they got lost for three hours trying to get a picture of the witch."

"Oh, no. That movie was so bad," Mollie laughs.

"Yeah, it's the worst. You can't see anything. Just a bunch of shadowy foliage," I say. "But the real party comes when someone brings out fireworks."

"You people set off fireworks?"

I laugh. "We totally do. Art kids love fireworks."

We make our way over to a group of kids I know from the one year I was in art. I may sing and write, but I can't draw a stick figure to save my life or my grade. These guys helped me fudge my art projects so they'd look halfway decent. I owe them my A- in mandatory Art I.

Mollie fits right in and pretty soon they're talking about artists I've never heard of. I know the greats like Picasso and that lady who painted all those flowers. But for the most part, art confuses me. Like modern art makes no sense. I went to the Guggenheim in New York once on my own accord because I was feeling cosmopolitan and adult. The main exhibit was just a room with walls covered in dollar bills. That was it. I could've done that and said it was a metaphor for the economy or consumerism, but would I have made it in the Guggenheim? No. My mom would just yell at me for putting staples in the wall.

"Do you like art, Carly?" Mollie asks.

I nod. "Big, big fan of Bob Ross."

The art kids chuckle and Mollie rolls her eyes, the sweetest smile spreading over her face.

"You're an idiot, Carly Allen," Mollie says.

"You're underappreciating Bob Ross, Mollie Fae," I say.

The art kids excuse themselves to join the dance party that's slowly growing, and it's just Mollie and me again.

"Want to go to the playground?" I ask, jerking my thumb toward the now vacant swings.

"Beat you there!" she says as she starts running.

"Hey!" I shout, chasing after her.

"You're so slow, Carly!" Mollie yells.

"You got a head start!" There's no way I'm catching up to this girl.

Mollie grabs a swing and turns around to see me still trailing. "Eat my shorts, Allen!"

I laugh as I slow down and make my way over to her. "Eat my shorts? Really?"

Mollie gestures at the playground, her smile glimmering in the moonlight. "I thought it was topical."

19

Fake Empire
by The National

"Do you know any of the constellations?" Mollie asks, taking a seat on the swing.

"Of course," I say. "You've got the belt one and the ladle ones and Hercules is up there somewhere."

Mollie laughs. "Just because it's in a Disney movie, doesn't mean there's actually a Hercules constellation."

"I'm serious!" I say. "He's really real. In the northern hemisphere from like spring to early winter."

Mollie twists the swing to look back at me. "Do you actually know what you're talking about?"

"Moderately," I shrug. "I like the stars and stuff. Space is crazy. There are explosions constantly and stars being born and black holes all going on up there. And we humans are like 'oh, three stars in a row means belt.'"

"Didn't people use them as maps?" Mollie asks.

"I think so, or maybe just the North Star. We don't give old, dead people enough credit," I say, kicking sand around.

"Swing with me?" Mollie asks.

"Nope," I say, shaking my head. "One time I flipped upside down one too many times at my grandparents' house and puked all over their azaleas. Haven't been on a swing since."

"Those poor azaleas."

"Actually, my grandfather said they grew better that year than any other year. He called my puke his special fertilizer."

Mollie gags and pulls a face. "Oh, gross."

Geez, Carly, you're taking this really potentially romantic moment and just puking all over it. Nope, that joke did not help to mask this embarrassment.

"Exactly," I say, clearing my throat. "So it's in everyone's best interest if I don't swing."

"That's fair," she says. "Push me, then?"

I walk behind Mollie's swing and pull on the chains. She leans so her back is pressed against my chest and I hold her there longer than I probably need to because I like how close she is to me. I let her go and she giggles as she starts flying. Her sandals have fallen off and her bare feet are kicking through the humid night air.

"Higher! Higher! Higher, Carly!" she yells.

I'm happy to oblige, pressing my hands to her back, using all my strength to send her as high as she wants to go. Her hair is flying and her laughter is bubbling and exploding, like when you stick a Mentos in a Diet Coke. Unavoidable, sweet, and impossible to contain. I never thought I'd compare a girl to a YouTube science experiment, but I guess there's a first time for everything. I laugh with her because I can't not.

After a while, Mollie digs her feet into the sand and comes to a stop. She twists to face me and I grab onto the chains to steady her. We're staring at each other and I think I might just have enough confidence to do what I really want to do.

All of a sudden, this moment is everything. This playground and us, it's all I can see. We're the only people on earth. The party's a million miles away, if it's even still there at all. Yeah, it's hot and humid because Maryland is an armpit of a swampy hellhole and I'm wearing jeans and a flannel shirt. My palms are sweaty and my hair has totally frizzed out. There are mosquitoes everywhere. But it's nice, being here tonight. Mollie's nice too. She's got her legs crossed, her elbows by her side. Her hair's a little messed up from all the wind when she was swinging. I can barely hear her breathing and she's not moving a muscle. It's almost like she's trying not to make any impact on the world, but that's foolish. We're all ripples in someone's pond. I move slowly, not totally surely, watching Mollie to see if she's moving toward me, too. I inhale just a little and I'm about to close my eyes when I hear someone frantically shouting my name.

"Carly! Carly! I found you a guitar, man," the kid from earlier says.

I groan and look over at him. "Oh, cool."

"Come play something for us," he says, shoving the guitar into my arms.

"Uh, yeah, I guess. Okay," I say, trying not to let my frustration come through.

"Do you know *Wonderwall?*" he asks.

Mollie starts laughing and I sigh. "Yeah, I know *Wonderwall.*"

"Come on!" he says, pulling me away.

I fucking hate *Wonderwall.*

20

We Built This City
by Starship

The band's been practicing for Cameron's End of Year Extravaganza for a while now, and actually playing music that's not One Direction has come with some challenges. We all have wildly different tastes in music. In a way, only playing One Direction was kind of a blessing. We started playing as a band because we all hated being in jazz band. Misery loves company, so we started messing around in Bryan's garage. Bryan's little sister wouldn't leave us alone until we played her a One Direction song. Then we realized how lucrative being a One Direction cover band in suburbia could be, and ta-da, the band was born. You could play a drinking game with the number of times I wrote One Direction in this paragraph.

The point is, we're struggling to find our image as a band. Bryan's really into death metal and, shockingly, I do not make a convincing lead singer of a screamo band. The twins love Adele and Joni Mitchell, which we can all agree on, but no one wants to spend the entire party crying over their exes. Heather says she doesn't really have an opinion about music, which confuses us all to no end. She doesn't even have any songs on her phone. I don't understand why she bothered to learn how to play the drums when she doesn't seem to care about music.

We've resorted to learning Top 40 songs we all hate, which means we're not as motivated as we should be. I'm singing half-heartedly, reading lyrics on my phone, and the band is squinting at badly photocopied sheet music. We're barely in tempo with each other and suddenly, the really good One Direction band has turned into a pretty awful high school jam band. We finish another song and I'm desperately hoping for a decent review.

"How was that?" I ask Claire, who looks up from her homework.

She shrugs. "I mean it was okay, but, y'know."

"No," I shake my head. "I don't know what that means."

"It's good, but now that you guys have changed things up, you're missing something," she says.

"Missing what?"

"Carly, chill. I don't have the answer. I'm just telling you what I feel."

"Ugh," I groan, sitting on an amp. "We have to play Cameron's party and we're aggressively mediocre."

"Mediocrity isn't bad," Heather says.

"Mediocrity is shit," Bryan says.

"We're not going to be a mediocre high school band," I say. "We were rock and roll before we started learning this." I gesture toward the sheet music for *Party in the U.S.A.* on Bryan's music stand.

"There's absolutely nothing rock and roll about a One Direction cover band, Carly. Let's get that settled now," Bryan says.

"Okay, well, *Party in the U.S.A.* I think is decidedly less rock and roll than One Direction. So tell me again why we aren't just playing One Direction."

Bryan looks at me incredulously. "First of all, their target demographic is pre-pubescent 12-year-olds who are hyperactive on Tumblr. Second, it's poppy bullshit. Third, this was your idea."

I shake my head. "Fuck you, Bryan. Our band is not just poppy bullshit. If it was, you wouldn't be here."

"Are you saying you want to break up the band?" Heather asks.

"No!" I exclaim. "Hell, no. I'm just saying we sound like shit. Do any of you think we're making anything good right now?"

"I think I liked One Direction more," Heather says.

"See!" I exclaim. "We at least liked One Direction."

"I didn't," Bryan mumbles.

"Shut it, Bryan," I say. "Yes, you did."

"So we change the set list?" one of the twins asks.

"I think we should," I say. "We should play the music we want to play. Music we like. Not the Top 40 songs they expect. We're not going to be any good that way."

"That seems too easy," Heather says.

"Yeah, we can't just play slightly more obscure Top 40 songs," Bryan grumbles.

"Why do we have to play contemporary stuff?" a twin asks.

I shake my head. "We're not about to branch into classical music."

"Not classical, just older popular songs that everyone knows," the other twin says. "Like *Teenage Dirtbag* or *My Own Worst Enemy*. Some Jack's Mannequin. Or even go into the '80s. Stuff people remember and that we like."

"That could work," Heather says.

"Why don't you write your own stuff?" Claire pipes up.

"That's a good question, Claire. Thank you," I say. "Why the hell don't we?"

"Uh, because we've never written a song before?" Bryan says.

"By that standard, no one would ever write a song," Heather chimes in.

"Why don't we try to make real music?" I ask, standing up. "We're all pretty competent musicians. Competent enough to be in a moderately successful cover band. So what's stopping us from creating real music?"

"What would we even sing about?" one of the twins asks.

"Whatever we want!" I say. I'm on a roll now. "We could sing songs about school or boys or girls. Life, you know? Just like Tom Petty and Springsteen and Joan Jett. I'm talking Chevy trucks, caramel sunsets, heartbreak, all of it."

"So we're a country band, now?" asks a twin. I really need to figure out who's who.

I think about it for a minute. "No, we'd be like pop Americana."

"Like if Bruce Springsteen and One Direction had a baby," the other twin says.

"One Direction aren't even American," Bryan says.

"Who's gonna write the words?" Claire asks.

"You need to be focusing on your practice test," I tell her. "But I think I've got enough melancholy young love for the whole the band."

"Matt and I are pretty good at writing music to lyrics," Mark offers sheepishly.

Finally. At long last I can tell these twins apart.

"We're really doing this?" Bryan asks with more sincerity than I've ever heard come out of his mouth.

The twins shrug in unison. "Why not?"

"I guess," Heather says.

I clap my hands. "Let's rock and roll."

Claire rolls her eyes. "Never say that again."

21

I Want You to Want Me
by Cheap Trick

"So, I hear you're in a band," Mollie says as I close my locker.

"Yeah. I thought the One Direction cover band was old news," I reply, turning to walk to my next class.

"Don't play dumb with me, Carly," she says, shoving my shoulder. "I heard you guys were writing real songs." Mollie stays close enough that with every step we take, our shoulders brush.

"Who told you such a ridiculous rumor?"

"Claire."

I sigh. "I keep forgetting you two are in the same gym class."

"So it's true?" Mollie asks.

"Well, I mean, kind of. Don't get too excited, though. We have no clue about how to write actual music."

"Who's writing the lyrics?" she asks, looking at me.

I look down. "Uh, that'd be yours truly."

"You always struck me as the thoughtful, artistic dreamer type."

"Hey, I'm pretty tough, thank you very much." I flex a bicep in meek demonstration.

"Claire also told me you guys bailed on band practice last week to go see *Zootopia* and you cried ten minutes in," Mollie says with a laugh.

"Oh my god," I groan. "You really have to stop hanging out with Claire. She's making me look so bad."

"So what are your songs about?" Mollie asks as we turn down the main hallway.

"You know, the usual. Girls, getting your heart broken. Falling in love. All that sensitive, artistic dreamer stuff," I say with a wink that exudes so much false confidence.

"Write any songs about me?" There goes all my confidence. False and real.

"Wh-why would I write, uh, you know. Why?"

She slaps me on the back. "Breathe, Carly. I'm kidding."

"Oh, I totally knew that," I say, forcing a laugh.

"I've never had anyone write a song about me."

I look at her. "Play your cards right and maybe you will."

"Speaking of playing my cards right," she says, "I heard you're a whiz at physics."

"I knew you were only using me for my brains."

"No. I'm using you for your good looks too."

"So you want me to tutor you in physics?" I ask, so casually ignoring her flirting that's getting too much for me to handle.

"It wouldn't be too bad," she says. "I'm sitting at a low B in standard physics and I need to get a C on the final to keep that B- afloat."

"Shouldn't be too hard," I say.

Mollie pats my shoulder. "Don't get all over-confident. I got a one out of eight on one of my quizzes."

"Alright, so an all-day study session?" I ask.

Mollie nods excitedly. "The Starbucks on the corner of the bypass on Saturday? Coffee's on me."

"Meet you there at ten."

"It's a date," Mollie says playfully. "A study date."

I laugh. "My favorite kind of date."

****

She was supposed to be here fifteen minutes ago. I already ordered without her and I've got my physics notes spread out around me. All the other people in Starbucks think I'm lying when I say that extra seat is reserved for someone. Honestly, I'm starting to not believe it myself.

Just when I think it's all over, when I'm trying to figure out how to sneak out of here in the least awkward way possible, Mollie comes rushing through the door. Her hair is piled up on top of her head, stringy and wet in one of those half-up, half-down hairstyles pretty girls can't get enough of. She's wearing an oversized flannel shirt that goes to her thighs and black skinny jeans. She sees me instantly.

"I'm so, so sorry about this," she says, dropping into the seat across from me.

"Oh, no, you're fine. No worries. I just got here, too," I say, and the guy at the table next to me snickers. How rude.

"You have a kid brother?" I shake my head no and she laughs. "I don't recommend getting one. Took him forever in the shower. Don't even want to think about what he does in there. He just turned fourteen. More power to him. He has a right to explore his sexuality, but he needs to do it on his own time and in his own room."

I laugh. "Well, I appreciate you showering for me."

She winks. "I aim to please." Suddenly she looks right at me and we get lost for a while.

I'm not good with words when it comes to my feelings and pretty girls. Articulacy aside, there's no way to truly explain this phenomenon. So y'all are going to have to humor me and attempt to put yourselves in my shoes. Okay, close your eyes.

WAIT!

Don't close your eyes because then you can't read these words. My bad. See? Off to a great start. Let's try this again.

Okay, so remember that first really overwhelming crush you had. Remember how you'd change your entire walking route to class just so you could run into them? How every little thing they did was amazing? Like the way they used to bite their pencil or the way they'd draw meaningless shapes in the margins of their notebook. That stuff got you good, didn't it?

Just stupid things you've seen hundreds of other humans do so many times. Suddenly, though, it's different. It's endearing and intoxicating and all-consuming. I still remember Stella Carraway and the way she used to smack her gum. In anyone else, it's an immensely infuriating habit, but Stella Carraway could've smacked gum right in my ear until the end of time and I would've thought it was the sweetest sound in the world. It's so dumb and it's all you can possibly think about.

Remember it? Like a tidal wave, huh? And then think about those times you'd sit across from them with no other distraction. Just them. When words became overwhelming and impossible and you'd just look at each other. There's something so youthful about having all the time in the world to just stare at another person. I know for a fact my parents are the most in love people on the planet, but I don't see them staring longingly into each other's eyes. Maybe they already have it memorized after so many years of being together. Maybe how long you spend looking into someone's eyes has no direct correlation to the success of a relationship.

Mollie Fae clears her throat and the magic ebbs. "Well, I'm going to order a latte with extra espresso. It'll be a miracle if you can get me to understand physics. I'm already tired just thinking about it."

I smile. "I'll be here."

22

Walking on Sunshine
by Katrina and the Waves

I know Madison's party is going to be a big deal when it's all anyone has talked about since I parked. While I walked from my parking spot to the front door of the school, I was stopped by no less than ten people telling me Madison was throwing a party. They insisted my attendance was beyond mandatory.

Now, and I feel like this is the case for most people, when someone tells me I *have* to do something or that it's *mandatory*, I lose all desire to do said thing. It's why all my homework is finished at the last second. The only reason it gets done at all is my crippling fear of failure and my desire to get out of Maryland.

By the time I get to my seat in first period, I've made up my mind that there's no way I'm going to Madison's party. I don't care that it'll be the best party of the year or that her dad works for Boone's Farm. No one likes Boone's Farm. I'm going to have a nice weekend where I don't get out of my pajamas until work on Saturday, then Claire and I will hang out later at the mall. But Sunday's all free. This feels like the weekend I finally finish *Gilmore Girls*. (Yeah, did you forget that I was watching that show? I didn't. Jess forever, Logan can shove it.)

"Hi, Carly," Annie says, taking her seat next to me. "Have you –"

I put my hand up. "Do not ask me if I've heard about Madison's party because I have and I'm not going."

"First of all, in what world would I have heard of a party before you? Second of all, did you skip your coffee this morning?"

I groan. "Not on purpose. I was in the drive-thru at Starbucks, I ordered my coffee, I tried to pay in all coins, and they rejected me."

"Carly Allen rejected. What is the world coming to?" Todd asks, sitting next to Annie and kissing her on the cheek.

"Watch it, bud. That's my best friend you're kissing. I can end you," I say. "I'm serious, though. Isn't that illegal?"

"Technically, yes, since coins are legal tender," Annie says.

"Exactly! But I didn't have it in me to argue because I hadn't had my coffee which I couldn't have because they wouldn't take my money," I say, exasperated. "It's a Möbius strip of suffering."

Todd laughs. "You'll be okay."

I glare at him. "Will I, Todd?"

"Ignore her, Todd," Annie says, scooting closer. "Now what's this I hear about a Maddisyn Hamilton party?"

I shake my head. "Madison Hope. So basically Maddisyn Hamilton except dial back on the Hot Topic vibes and send money and preppiness through the roof. That's only scratching the surface of Madison Hope."

"Was 1998 the year of Madisons?" Todd asks.

"My middle name's Madyson with an M and a Y," Annie says. "And you're not going? That's wildly uncharacteristic of you."

"I don't know. Everyone's telling me to go and they're saying it's going to go down in Towson High School history. She doesn't even have a pool, so that seems highly unlikely."

"Oh," Annie says. "So it has nothing to do with the fact that Mollie Fae is one of Madison's best friends and she hasn't invited you despite the fact that the two of you had the greatest study date of all time this weekend?"

"Why do I tell you anything?" I ask, flustered. "Don't be ridiculous."

"I'll stop when you stop," Annie shoots back.

"You should go, though, Carly," Todd pipes up. "I mean, if Madison and Mollie are such great friends, there's a good chance Mollie will be there, right?"

"Yeah," Annie adds. "What he said. Isn't my boyfriend smart?"

"Gross," I say, then smile. "I don't know. I doubt I'll go. The thought of having an almost entirely free weekend sounds wonderful to me."

"No hot dates on the horizon?" Annie asks.

"Yeah, with Scott, the cash register, and Claire. Three of the hottest dates a girl can ask for," I say as Mr. Hall comes in.

"Listen up. Before we start today, it's finally that point in the semester. Time to vote for class speaker," he says, holding up a stack of half sheets of paper.

Class speaker is basically the cool equivalent of valedictorian. Teachers nominate five kids from the graduating class as potential speakers. It's usually the most academically savvy popular ones who get nominated. All the nominees pretend it's *sooo* embarrassing and they beg their friends not to vote for them when that's actually all they really want. It's the ultimate high school popularity contest. Winning over the teachers and the students is quite a feat.

When Mr. Hall drops the voting sheet on my desk, I'm genuinely shocked to see my own name staring back at me.

"Way to go, Carly," Annie whispers as she puts a check next to my name.

A few kids turn to look at me when they see my name

listed there. They give me knowing looks and winks before making marks on their papers.

My first thought should be about pride or something since this is such an honor, but my mind's gone straight to Mollie Fae. Shocker, right? I can't help but wish I knew what crossed her mind when she saw my name there.

"Pass 'em in! It doesn't take that long to make one check mark," Mr. Hall says.

I quickly put a check next to my name, because why not. I'm not above voting for myself. I'll admit that it could be fun to make a speech in front of everyone. Oh, but wait! I'd actually have to write something personal and read it in front of a whole bunch of people. Is it too late to take back my vote?

"Now that we have that out of the way," Mr. Hall says, rubber banding the votes together, "let's talk *Mrs. Dalloway.*"

I spend the rest of class zoning out. I already finished *Mrs. Dalloway.* It's a quick read, but a little dry. I skimmed it, though, so maybe I missed something. I don't know if you've caught on, but I'm a little distracted at the moment. Based on the other terrible books we've had to read this year, I doubt I'm wrong.

The bell rings and I'm the last one out the door, struggling to get my books together. Who's that I see standing against the lockers looking all pretty? Mollie Fae.

Of course it is. Geez, can't this girl ever give me a second to breathe.

I walk up to her, smiling. "Come to the English hallway often?"

She bites her lip. "I made you a mixtape."

"Wait, really? I thought you forgot about that."

"Of course I didn't forget," she says, putting the cassette in my hands. "Here, like I promised. Songs for you to cry to."

I laugh. "Yeah, thank you for this. And thanks for all the little drawings." She's decorated the cassette with storm clouds and frowning faces. "They really set the vibe. I'm going to listen to this as soon as I get home." I put the tape in my backpack. "Walk you to class?"

She links her arm with mine. "Lead the way."

We round the corner into the science hallway and she says, "I voted for you."

"Really?" She nods. "You think I'd write a good speech?"

"I kinda just want you to get up there and sing a One Direction medley."

I laugh. "You're so desperate to hear me sing, aren't you? Just come to one of our shows."

"I tend to not be invited to many bat or bar mitzvahs," she says.

"What about ten-year-olds' birthday parties?"

"Shockingly, not many of those on my social calendar either."

I shrug. "Tough break, then. Although there's a rumor we'll be playing Cameron's End of Year Extravaganza."

"Well, I guess I'll have to attend then. Speaking of parties and social calendars," she says, looking up at me, "is yours open this weekend? There's this party I'm going to and I wanted to know if you were going too."

"Oh, yeah?" I'm holding my breath.

She nods. "Madison Hope's. It's a massive mansion party while her parents are away fixing their marriage by having affairs."

"That sounds healthy."

"You want go with me? I know it's a step down from your bat mitzvahs, but I think you'll have fun if you come."

"Yes," I say, letting out the breath I forgot I was holding.

"Cool," she says slowly, elongating that one syllable.

"Cool," I say, just as slowly, but nowhere near as coolly.

"Well, this is my stop," Mollie says, gesturing to the physics classroom. "I guess I'll see you Friday night. Or sooner."

"You most definitely will see me, Mollie Fae," I say, my suave, casual grin threatening to run wild.

"Looking forward to it, Carly Allen," she says, giving my arm a squeeze as she walks away.

I wave and lean against the lockers. I let gravity and an overwhelming happiness pull me to the ground. I watch the shoes of my classmates shuffle by, some small part of my brain vaguely aware that I have a class on the other side of the school to get to. The rest of my brain is planning a flash mob of pure joy singing and dancing to *Walking on Sunshine*.

The one-minute warning bell rings and I scramble to my feet. I sprint down the almost empty hallways and it all feels so wonderfully sublime. I'm dancing in the science hallway. Gene Kelly's got nothing on me.

23

I Need a Woman
by Noah Gundersen

When I get home, I pull out the Walkman I bought for a dollar at a yard sale a few years ago. My fingers trace over the drawings on the cassette case. The storm clouds and frowny faces are too goofy for what she insists are truly heartbreaking songs. I check the back for a track listing, but it's just more frowny faces.

I put the cassette in and close the lid. Mollie's voice comes through loud and clear.

"Hi, Carly Allen. You're the only person in the world who still has a cassette player and I'm the world's best mixtape maker." She pauses and the volume's up so loud I can hear her take a deep breath. "So I guess it's a good thing we found each other." Then there's silence again through the headphones and I'm acutely aware of how loudly my heart's beating.

"Anyway," she says softly, "these are the saddest songs I know, and I think you've got enough sadness in you to fully appreciate them. Oh!" She gasps, and I smile because I know the face she's making and the way her hands are clasped. "I forgot. My favorite song ever is on here. See if you can figure out which one it is. Good luck."

With that, she's gone and replaced by a man who sounds like Ryan Adams if Ryan Adams had a bit more vocal training. So far, Mollie's right about the fact that this man is sad. I can picture him now: grungy clothes, guitar sagging, standing on a dirty, dim bar stage. I close my eyes and listen to this sad man sing his sad, sad songs.

Only they aren't that sad at all. I mean, probably every other person who listens to this guy hears his indie orchestrations and heartbreaking lyrics and it's sad. Not me though. All I can think about is Mollie in her room with her boom box. Sitting there at her desk, hearing the same songs I'm hearing now.

The first song Emma and I ever danced to was *Good Vibrations* by The Beach Boys, which is objectively the happiest song in the world. It came on the radio once when we were home alone in my room. She thought it sounded hokey, so I made her get up and dance. I remember we were alone because the school day had turned into an early release snow day and my parents were still out. Whenever I hear that song, I remember dancing in my room with a pretty girl as the first snow of the season fell, and it just makes me so sad.

These songs have stories for Mollie. They have meaning, and maybe she's cried while listening to them, but these songs make me feel so happy. Like I could reach the moon right now. Reach up and pluck it right out of the sky and put it in my room. Play hopscotch on the stars and miss a square. I know I should be sad, but I'm listening to these songs picked just for me by a pretty girl. This guy's singing about having his heart torn to pieces, doused in lighter fluid, and set on fire, and I feel like my heart's alive for the first time in the better part of a year.

I know which song's her favorite instantly.

> It's Cigarettes isn't it?

The response is immediate.

> You're good at this...which one did you like?

> I'm partial to I Need a Woman

I'm suddenly feeling brave. The three typing dots appear, then disappear, quickly squashing any ounce of that newfound bravery I had.

The response that finally comes through makes me catch my breath.

You've got a woman Carly

And then...

Doggy Ray Cyrus hasn't stopped
whining about you since you
visited

I let my head bang on my desk because of course I'm
that much of an idiot to read too much into song titles.

Why did I not know Doggy Ray
Cyrus was a girl?

Don't be so heteronormative
Carly. Girls can be named Billy
Ray Cyrus

Hahaha true but should anyone
really be named after Billy Ray
Cyrus?

Carly Allen you take that back
right now. Doggy Ray Cyrus is
proud of her name and did
nothing to deserve that

Here

I type that one word and then take a quick fifteen
selfies of my best apologetic face. It takes me a while to
pick the right one. I'm a nervous, shallow person. Sue me
for wanting to look cute for this girl I might possibly have a
crush on.

Show that to Doggy Ray Cyrus.
Tell her I'm sorry.

Then it's radio silence for a while. Maybe I shouldn't
have sent a selfie. Are we not selfie level friends right now?
Is this why old people hate millennials, because being selfie
level friends is something I'm worried about?

A picture comes through of Mollie smiling and Doggy
Ray Cyrus, freshly coneless, proudly licking Mollie's cheek.
It's the cutest thing I've ever seen.

> Totally gonna put that on Instagram.
> Woman crush Wednesday

Two can play at this ambiguous flirting game, Mollie Fae.

> That's a little presumptuous don't you think?

> Check Instagram

I quickly post the picture with the caption "Woman Crush Wednesday goes out to this cutie. Doggy Ray Cyrus + Carly 5ever."

> You're ridiculous

My phone buzzes with a text from Claire.

> How obsessed with this girl are you?

I shoot back.

> Get off Instagram and do your
> bio homework

Claire just sends the middle finger emoji back.

Then I get a text from Annie with a screenshot of my Instagram post.

> Oh, honey, you've got it really
> bad

I laugh and toss my phone onto the bed behind me, then turn my attention back to the cassette player and rewind the tape. That sad, sad man continues to sing and all of a sudden, I have a desire to write something.

24

What I Like About You
by The Romantics

"Now who's the uncool weirdo who wants to get to the party on time?" Annie asks from behind me.

"Yeah, haha, get all those I told you so comments out of your system now, okay?" I say, buttoning up my shirt.

"Why? Don't want to be embarrassed in front of your date?"

"How's this look?"

"You're joking, right?" Annie asks. "You're wearing a button up and black jeans, which is what you wear every single day."

I shrug. "Yeah, but these are new black jeans."

"Oh, yes, now I see. The knees are the tiniest bit less frayed."

"Jerk."

She laughs. "Is this how dramatic I was when I went out with Todd the first time?"

"Worse," I say, and start unbuttoning my shirt.

"What're you doing?"

"If I really do wear this outfit every single day, it's not going to impress her, so I'm going to change."

"Oh, no you're not," Annie says, getting up from the bed.

"You're not the boss of me."

"Hey, hey, look at me," she says, hugging me from behind.

I let my head fall back against her shoulder and look at the two of us in the mirror.

"You are Carly Allen. A girl so great, your parents needed two first names to name you."

I smile at her.

"I can guarantee that your future with Mollie does not hinge on your wardrobe, and I think if you showed up in a terrible denim suit straight out of the early 2000s, she'd still be into you," she says and lightly kisses my cheek, then smacks my behind. "Now let's go get 'em!"

"I can't believe you just slapped my ass."

She shrugs. "You have a nice ass. Don't act weird. I've told you this before. My only complaint about Todd is that he doesn't have the ass of a woman."

****

Todd finds Annie the second we arrive and I know she feels guilty about leaving me on my own, but I send them

167

on their way. I probably have a solid hour before Mollie shows up, so I make my way into the kitchen to grab a drink.

"Only beer and wine coolers? Is this a joke?" I ask, rummaging through the cooler.

"Afraid not," I hear a girl say behind me, and instantly I'm fourteen years old again.

"Stella Carraway," I say, standing up.

"Charlotte Maureen Allen."

"I told you that in total secrecy when we were fourteen! I'm honestly shocked you still remember."

"How could I forget my first kiss? I've got to tell my kids about you someday," she says, reaching down to pull out a wine cooler.

"Oh, yeah."

She crosses her arms. "That's all you have to say to me? I gave you my youth, Carly Allen."

I laugh. "Ah, yes, the summer before freshman year. The best time of our lives."

"I should hope so," she smiles.

"So what have you been up to? You go to some private school now, right?"

She nods. "Yep, Friends. Graduation's coming next, then summer, then UCLA."

"Wow, look at you go. All the way out to California."

"What about you, Carly?" she asks as she takes a sip.

"Uh, well, I'm not sure," I say, looking down and scuffing my shoes on the ground.

"You aren't sure? You were the most confident fourteen-year-old I knew. What the hell happened?"

"Some pretty girl broke my heart on a playground four years ago."

She shakes her head. "If I remember correctly, I was the one who ended up running home crying."

"Yeah, I'm really sorry about that." I scratch the back of my neck.

She waves me off. "Years of therapy have helped me move on. I'm serious, though. Did you apply to any schools?"

"Sure. I got rejected from some and got into some. I just haven't decided, you know?"

She nods. "I'm sure you'll figure it out."

"Yeah, eventually I have to."

"Who'd you come here with?" she asks, looking around.

"Oh, um Annie. You remember Annie, right? She and Todd are together. I guess he's her boyfriend officially. Todd Glass. And I'm waiting for Mollie Fae," I say, hopefully super smoothly, but Stella catches on remarkably quickly.

"You and Mollie Fae, huh?" she asks, eyes twinkling.

"What?" I say, flustered. "No, like as a friends thing."

"Carly, I'm not an idiot and neither are you. She's cute. We took dance together for a while when we were younger. You done good," she says, ruffling my hair.

I wave her hand away. "Who'd you come with?"

"Audrey, because she's dating the guy whose sister's throwing this party, whoever that is," she says.

"Stella!" We both turn to see who I presume is Audrey, waving her down.

"Speak of the devil," Stella says, grabbing another wine cooler. "One for the road."

I laugh as she makes her way toward Audrey. "It was good to see you, Stella Carraway."

She turns back around, walks up to me, and kisses me on the cheek. It's a little wet and I know there'll be a lipstick stain when she pulls away.

"You'll figure it all out." She winks at me. "I know that for certain."

Well, at least someone is certain about something in my life. With a quick kiss to my other cheek, she's gone.

I look back in the cooler in the hope that somehow something better ended up in there, but it's still just the same. There has to be stronger alcohol somewhere in this house and I'm going to find it.

Kids are everywhere. Making out on the couch, playing beer pong on an upside down painting, getting high on the staircase. Some of them I know and some are like Stella's friend, just distant acquaintances in search of easily accessible alcohol.

The basement is populated by computer kids. They're playing *Halo* or *Call of Duty* or who knows which war video game. They give me a nod and let me continue on my search and there, deep in a back corner, is a bottle of whiskey.

My phone says it's still early and this whiskey says it's time to get tipsy, so I plop down on the couch and watch them play.

"I'm going to do a shot every time one of you dies," I say.

A kid with a buzz cut laughs. "You got a death wish?"

"Are you guys good at this game?" I ask, as a character walks onto a land mine and gets blown sky-high. I take a swig.

The buzz cut kid talks again. "I am, but Jeremy sucks."

The kid I presume to be Jeremy scoffs. "Do not."

A girl sitting cross-legged on the floor pipes up. "You really do."

I raise my bottle to them. "Right on."

25

I Wanna Dance with Somebody (Who Loves Me)
by Whitney Houston

It turns out they're worse than awful at that game and now I'm more than a little tipsy. Maybe I'm full-on drunk. I'm in the living room with a bottle of beer dancing my heart out to One Direction. Stella's friend Audrey has made herself the DJ. As I've said before, I dance like a nerdy father, but when One Direction or Taylor Swift comes on, I am unstoppable.

Hours and hours have passed and it's after midnight, but I haven't seen Mollie Fae yet. Granted, I haven't really looked that hard, so maybe I should do that.

I start in the kitchen so I can get another beer. Beer, I'm discovering, tastes better when you're already drunk. Other than that, it tastes like expired bread that's been left outside in the garbage during the hottest days of summer.

She's not in the kitchen or the line for the bathroom or the off-limits bedrooms. She's not in the front yard or the side yard or the alley. I finally find myself on the back porch and Mollie Fae is nowhere to be found.

That's fine, I guess. I mean it is her life and she can choose to live it however she wants. She didn't have to come to this party, even though she invited me. Even if she didn't invite me, I'd still be here. Annie would've dragged me or Stella Carraway would've texted me out of the blue, begging me to keep her company. It has to be fine. There's no other option because she's not here.

I look out into the yard to see if I recognize anyone I want to talk to, and who do I see but Emma. Emma, standing in the middle of the yard, laughing. Emma, who was a gigantic asshole to me. Emma, whose number my fingers were just mindlessly dialing on my phone, which is what always happens when I'm drunk and lonely. Emma, who by some shocking turn of events, is the one who's here.

Seeing her sets off firecrackers in my stomach. Not like the ones I get when I see Mollie Fae. These aren't bright or warm. They're like getting punched over and over and over. Rolling punches I'm too beaten down to take. Her number is staring at me from my phone, encouraging me to do something. Anything. Any other night I could put my phone away and keep drinking, but she's here. The difference between ten numbers on a screen and an actual person utterly astounds me.

173

You think you remember when you're dialing their number. You think you remember every ounce of their being and their aura, but all you can remember is cardboard. Stiff cardboard cutouts that play out memories in your mind and pose for photos hidden away in shoeboxes under beds. No one warns you. Her hair is marvelously golden, her eyes shine brighter than a star, her legs are longer and smoother. My heart is a thoroughbred, clamoring to sprint down the miracle mile to the Technicolor girl in front of me.

I hate her.

I hated her this morning. I've hated her every single day since we broke up. In one second, it's like every shitty memory has been digitally remastered. One second and my feet are walking over to her and my brain, my stupid drunk brain, thinks this is a stunning idea. Here she is. Alive and real and within my reach. It's a game changer. Flip the board on its end and throw out the rules.

"Carly Allen, where the hell have you been?"

I know that smile. I know it's the smile she gets when she believes she has the upper hand. I'm two smiles away from being down for the count. Completely smashed under her finger. Two smiles and I'll be a goner.

"Here, there. You know, everywhere," I slur, waving my beer. It's pathetic.

She smiles. That's one. "Hmm," she bites her lip and

my eyes drop. I remember doing that to her myself. I take a big drink. "Funny, I haven't seen you anywhere."

I shrug. "Guess you haven't been looking in the right places."

"Well, looks like I finally made it," and she caps it off with a smile. For all you folks playing at home, that's two. It didn't take long at all.

I'm sure I could walk away from her. Ignore her like I blocked her number, but it doesn't matter. Her number's blocked, but I have it memorized. I hate her, but here she is. I can smell her perfume that used to linger everywhere. In my car, on my shirt, on sweatshirts she stole and I had to steal back. Now it's swirling around me like a heavy haze. If I breathe deeply enough, I can time travel. I can go back to before it all went so wrong.

It would be so easy to just give in, especially tonight. She's wearing that dress I've always liked and I'm pushing her pretty, pretty hair behind her ears like I've done so many times. I don't want to worry about what she's thinking or why she's looking at me like that, but it's too late. Those looks and her thoughts consumed me for the better part of a year. Even if I don't want to, I know them without a doubt and I know where they're leading us.

Do I still want Emma? No. No, that's not it at all. It's because I am so far from being fine. It's because Mollie Fae isn't here. Everyone is partnered up and cuddled up. It's the end. We're all friends again. Past hatred has been swapped for sentimentality. I see all the kids mingling and being and living and she's not here. Mollie Fae isn't here like she said she would be. Do I wish it was her standing in front of me? Absolutely. If she walked through that door right now, at this very instant, I would drop it all. Change my mind and tell her everything I've been too afraid to say to her face.

But I'm drunk. And I'm so, so lonely and here's this pretty girl standing right in front of me. She took my heart once before and utterly massacred it, but I don't care. I don't care that Mollie Fae isn't here. She's not the reason I came to this stupid party anyway. She's not the reason I actually brushed my hair and made an effort to look good tonight. She's not. She can't be because she's not here.

Emma is here, though. I can pretend those firecrackers in my gut are like they used to be. I can pretend this girl is the right choice because the right choice isn't here to make me think otherwise.

I let my cup drop and I feel the beer wet my pants by my ankles. I grab the fabric of her dress on her hips and pull her toward me. She smiles. One more smile to seal the deal.

"I think we should go somewhere quiet, Carly," she whispers.

For a moment, I'm gone. In one fleeting moment of sober clarity, I recognize the terrible decision I'm making. I see a flash of brown hair moving through the crowd and I think I'm saved. My knight in shining summer dress and flannel is here to save the day. And I don't even care that she'll find me with my hands on some other girl's hips. Anything, everything can be explained if I can get out of this. But no, it's Amber from government. My moment's over. I look at Emma and I hate how easy it is to be with her again.

I pull her closer until I feel her breath lightly tickle my lips. "I'd like that."

26

Wonderwall
by Ryan Adams

People always say that waking up with a hangover is like having a jackhammer in your head. Right now, it feels like there's an entire construction site inside my skull. A cacophony of bulldozers, cranes, and old dudes yelling, and I just want to find a wrecking ball and make it all stop.

I feel Emma cuddling into me and it all comes down.

Shit.

I check under the blankets.

Double shit.

There are many ways last night should've gone and this is certainly not what I wanted or anticipated. And Madison's parents' bed of all places. I quickly gather up my discarded clothes. One sock is MIA, but the construction site gets louder and louder with every move I make. I just need to get out of here.

As I sneak out of the bedroom, I silently pray I don't run into anyone in Madison's family. I'm trying to avoid the conversation that goes something like "Hi, Mr. Madison's Dad, sorry I had sex in your bedroom and the girl I had sex with is still in there, but you don't have to yell at me, I already realize how stupid it was."

"Carly!"

I turn around and sure enough, standing at the end of the hallway in the kitchen is Mollie Fae. Smiling like the sun, making the construction site even louder. I give her a wave.

She starts walking quickly toward me. "I've been thinking about doing this a lot since the other night and I'm not going to think about it anymore. To hell with it, I'm just going to do it."

I'm halfway to half a cohesive thought when Mollie's arms wrap around my neck and she's kissing me. Mollie Fae is kissing me, Carly Allen. That's one for the history books, kids.

I drop the shoes in my hand and they clatter to the floor. My hands slide around her waist, bunching up her shirt as they make their way around. I feel the little divots at the bottom of her spine and she shivers as I let my fingers slowly crawl across her lower back. She tastes like toothpaste and the first real thought my brain has is how my mouth probably tastes. Probably like something died in it last night. Thankfully, Mollie doesn't seem to mind.

Her hands are in my hair and I pull her tighter, tighter,

tighter. I can't get her close enough. She's sunshine and a long sunset. The moon and all of the stars. She's Disneyland on a school day and an everlasting autumn. She's like the first taste of soda pop on the first official day of summer vacation.

You know movie reviewers and the weird shit they say when they talk about actors? Like a world-stopping transformation, or a miraculous, extraordinary vision. Just like a bunch of out-of-the-box adjectives strung together. I think that's how we should talk about people in real life. I'm no professional movie reviewer, but I've seen *Citizen Kane*, so that has to count for something. Mollie is a spectacular, startling, enigmatic revelation. A marvelous, spellbinding dream that I want to go on and on.

But it ends. She's pulling away, eyes droopy. I'm not much better. We're both smiling stupid smiles. She giggles and hides her face in my neck.

"What are you doing here so early?"

I grimace, remembering now how this chance encounter came to be. I try to close Madison's parents' door behind me. "Haha, or late. Better crash than crash."

She pulls away a little, and her eyes look through the cracked door. I see them harden for just a moment. I know what she sees in there. Emma's bare back and tangled sheets on the bed I spent the night in.

I cough a little. "So, missed you at the party last night."

She cocks an eyebrow and takes a few steps back. "Emergency family game night was imposed and I couldn't get out of it."

I nod. "Things get out of hand?"

"That appears to be the theme of the night. One of us certainly had a little more fun than the other."

Then she laughs. It's not happy and it's not joyful. It's nauseating and it turns my stomach inside out. "You know, Carly? You make yourself out to be this innocent hopeless romantic and it's so clear that you desperately want to be in love and I'm not trying to be presumptuous and say we should fall in love, but you kissed me back!" Her fingers are scraping back her hairline, tensing into fists. "You kissed me back just now! Like a good, proper kiss. What the hell was that about? I feel like such an idiot." She squares her stance and says, "You know, I really thought after all of this...do you even like me, Carly?"

Yes. Oh my god, yes. Yes, a million and one times. Yes, Mollie, I like you a lot. Yes, yes, yes. I like the way you laugh. I like the way your hair falls from its bun one strand at a time and I've thought a thousand times over about what it would be like to run my fingers through it. I love the freckles on your nose and the fact that you only have one dimple. I like how you sang under your breath that one time we did homework together. I like all the things I don't even know about you yet and I like that I could have the chance to get to know them. Yes, yes, yes, I do. I do like you, Mollie.

But nothing's coming out of my mouth. All of that is whizzing around in my brain, desperate to tumble out, to explain it all, but my jaw's locked and I don't have the key. It's like there's an angel banging on my brain telling me to just say it all. To open the floodgates and he promises I'll be able to walk on water. I won't drown. The angel's kicking and screaming and I am so, so close. Poor angel's trying his hardest, but the devil in front of him isn't budging.

She shakes her head. "I really thought I was prepared for every possible outcome."

"Mollie, wait," I say as she starts to leave.

She turns, shaking all over. "I think you should go. Madison's parents are going to be home any minute."

And then she's gone, walking down the hallway. I want my legs to catch up to my heart and run after her. I want to run, hair flying in the wind like they do in all the movies. I want to spin her around and say "It's always been you" and then kiss her again. Kiss her so she can forget what she just saw and believe in me. But nothing's moving. I'm not going anywhere. I can't. She wants nothing to do with me and it's all my fault.

****

The drive back to my house is dismal. The construction site in my head is louder than ever and the sun is so, so bright, but I don't feel warm at all. I say hi to my parents when I walk into the kitchen, and I'm sure they can tell I just spent the last twelve hours drinking and making terrible decisions. Hopefully I look tragic enough that they'll pity me instead of punish me.

In the safety of my room, I flop face down on my bed. I should call Annie. Maybe she can help make something positive come out of this experience, but my phone's dead somewhere on the floor and I am not moving. I hear a knock on the door.

"Hey, Carly," my mom says quietly.

I grunt back.

"Annie called and said you were spending the night and for us not to worry." I feel the bed give a little as she sits down.

I need to remember to thank Annie at some future point in time for helping me out. What a stellar friend.

"Something tells me you weren't at Annie's, though."

Uh, oh.

"I mean, Annie was there," I struggle out.

"I do commend you for not drinking and driving."

"I wasn't – "

"You can't fool me, Carly. I, too, had fun once upon a time behind my parents' backs."

I huff. "I wouldn't say it was fun."

"Yeah, hangovers are no good, but I've got Dad cooking you some breakfast and there's coffee in the pot. Scientifically, only time can reduce your blood alcohol content, but some people claim greasy food helps."

"You lost me after coffee."

I hear her laugh lightly. "Do you want to talk about what else is bothering you?"

I feel the knot in my throat, the telltale sign I'm about to cry. "Just girl stuff, you know. No big deal."

"We all know that's a lie. Nothing involving a girl is ever a small thing."

I really can't get into this today. "Trust me, it's not a big deal."

"If you say so," she says, and pulls me into a hug. "Now brush your teeth, go downstairs, and get some breakfast. You have work in an hour."

I groan dramatically. "Way to ruin my already terrible morning, Mom."

She stands up and laughs. "I'm not the one who decided to have a turbulent social life."

27

Come See About Me
by The Supremes

It turns out the only thing worse than having a hangover is having to go to work with a hangover. I roll into Spin Me, Baby only five minutes late with an extra-large coffee from the Starbucks across the street. I don't know what ridiculous name the extra-large is called, but it's extra and it's large and supposedly bigger than the human stomach, which is everything I need right now. Scott's the only other person in the store and he greets me by shouting my name.

"Hi, Scott," I yell back, wincing. It's going to be a long shift.

"What's with the sunglasses indoors? Your future too bright?" he asks as he walks up to the register where I intend to sit for the entire shift.

"More like future too shitty." Scott likes it when I swear. Says it keeps him young. I would want to feel young too if I was pushing 3,000 years old.

"Ahh, girl trouble?" Why does he keep shouting?

I just nod and drink a quarter of the coffee in one gulp.

Scott winks at me. "You know, one time I knew this girl, Betsy something or other. We sat next to each other on a plane and I decided to ditch my plans and go to her brother's wedding as her date, even though we'd just met. Here's my advice for you, Carly. Never go to a wedding in Florida. All of Betsy's family got so drunk they forgot who I was and tried to feed me to the gators. Never date Floridians, Carly, if you can help it. They're real good in the sack, though, you know what I mean?" He laughs, jabbing me with his elbow. I think I'm going to vomit.

"It's crazy how similar our lives are," I yell back, praying this all ends soon.

He whistles. "I knew I liked you, kid. You're kind of a son to me."

I'm too hungover to deal with that comment, so I just let him walk back to his office. Scott's the one in charge of taking in all the used records, appraising them, and pricing them. It seems pretty arbitrary to me, but he insists the records speak to him. I think he's just high 24/7. One time, he called me into his office when we were slammed during the Christmas season. He held a Paul Anka record to my ear and asked me what it was saying. I stared at him and said nothing because it's just a record. He shook his head and said, "I thought you were ready." I want to be him when I'm ninety-seven. Crazy, constantly high as a kite, and owner of a moderately successful record store.

Scott doesn't care what I play, so I put on a '60s compilation album, starting with *It's My Party* by Lesley Gore. I hear the bell above the door chime and who walks in but Zoe. Zoe, as in the reason Emma and I broke up Zoe. She looks like hell and that's being quite generous. She's wearing a sweatshirt and baggy sweatpants, despite the fact that it's nearing summer in Maryland and it's hot outside. I push my sunglasses to the top of my head so I can get a better look. Her face is all red and puffy and things start clicking in my disastrously hungover brain.

As if my sleeping with Emma couldn't get any more monumentally horrible, I think I just ruined Zoe's life. I made my ex cheat on the girl who made that same ex cheat on me. Is that right? Doesn't matter. This is too convoluted and incestuous for me. I feel like I might vomit. I did this. I'm no better than Emma.

I watch Zoe wander around the store a little longer, pausing every once in a while to wipe her eyes. I feel horrible terrible awful. But maybe something else is wrong in her life, like maybe her grandma died.

No, I should not be rooting for a dead grandmother scenario. I'm a terrible human. She's probably here to kick my ass like I deserve. I see her collecting a stack of records.

Poor kid got her heart broken and she's going to drop at least $100 on records to cry the heartbreak away. Finally, she makes her way to the register.

I clear my throat. "Find everything okay?"

She just nods as I start scanning. "Uh, actually, you don't have Taylor Swift's *Red* album, do you?" Her voice is all distorted and I know it's my fault.

Twist the knife in my gut, why don't you? "No, sorry. We just sold out last week, but we've got some coming in soon. Want me to put your name down?"

She pushes her hair back, shakes her head, and gives me a smile that reminds me of those sad Sarah McLachlan dog commercials. The vinyls she picked aren't much better. Every Taylor Swift album except *Red*, Sam Smith, Joni Mitchell's *Blue*, and Adele's *19, 21,* and *25.* That's the starter pack for crying alone in your room with a quart of Ben & Jerry's.

"So, are you okay? These are some sad, sad albums."

She looks down at her shoes. "I got cheated on, so I've had better days.

I nod my head. I should tell her it was me. Tell her I'm the reason she feels like she's been run over by all eighteen wheels of a tractor trailer. Let her get in one good punch to help her out in the short run. But I'm not much on bravery.

"Been there. Bitches, right?" I say as I finish scanning the albums.

She looks at me funny. "How'd you know it was a girl?"

"Lesbian intuition," I say. "Also, it'll be $60 even for the albums."

She nods and hands me her credit card. I pass her the bag of her records.

"Listen, it feels pretty awful to start with, but I think you're going to be okay," I say in an effort to help her. Or maybe I want to make myself feel better. I give her back her card and receipt.

"Thanks," she says, and as she's turning to leave I see her eyes getting all watery again.

It's just me alone in the store now. I can't help it. I feel tears coming so I put my sunglasses back on to try and maintain my sense of composure. It only makes the tears come faster. I don't even know if I'm crying for Zoe or for myself because I remember being in her shoes or for Mollie because of what I've done to her. Regardless, I finally vomit.

28

You Don't Know How It Feels
by Tom Petty

I'm sure I look like the poster child for appalling decisions when I show up at the mall food court in sunglasses, holding another extra-large coffee, and probably smelling of vomit. Claire and I are supposed hang out and I can't let her down too. She wants to see some rom-com, in a weird turn of events, and I end up sleeping through it. Could probably tell you how it ends though. The guy gets the girl. How nice it must be to be the guy in a rom-com. You always, always, always get the girl. Claire has to shake me awake as the credits roll. We end up in the food court, cheese fries between us.

"You're weird, Carly," Claire says, taking a loud slurp of her soda.

"Thank you."

"Before I met you, I thought you were like all the other popular kids. Dumb, rich, and uninteresting, but you're not."

"Thank you? Again?"

"You're none of those things, so I had no clue how a smart, not rich lesbian got popular. No offense," she says, and I just shrug. "So I started watching you in the halls."

"That's creepy," I groan.

"Whatever. I think it's because you're so confident that people are drawn to you."

I'm a little taken aback by her sincerity. "Uh, thank you. For real this time."

"But you're not confident," she says.

"Wow, okay, I take back all my thanks." I'm slightly annoyed.

"You've got some confidence, but it's fake confidence. Like you're a good lead singer and you put on this whole act on stage. Pretend like you don't give a shit. It works. You do it at school, too," she says, brushing her hair behind her ear. "Do you know what I mean?"

"No."

She thinks for a moment. "You're good with crowds, but not with people."

I lean back in my chair and cross my arms. "Where is all this coming from?"

She shrugs. "My therapist says I'm good at reading people. It's kind of like a hobby."

"Lovely."

"I'm serious about you, though. You're happy all the

time. That's why you're so popular. You're just Happy Gilmore all the time."

"You do know that Happy Gilmore was actually super angry, right?"

"But then," she continues indifferently, "when you talk to that hot, nerdy girl, you're like 30% there. All that confidence goes poof."

"What's your point?" I ask.

She sips her soda. "No point, I guess. Just thought you'd want to know."

"Cool. Wonderful. Thank you for highlighting that flaw," I say.

"So you know your confidence is fake?"

"No shit," I say.

"Why won't you just ask that girl out? Are you a bad kisser?"

"No, I'm a fine kisser. Not that it's any of your business," I say, running my hands through my hair. "Besides, I think it's a deeper issue than that."

Claire whistles. "Sounds like you need a therapist."

I shake my head. "No thank you."

"Carly Allen's too good for therapy?"

"No," I sigh. "I just hate talking to people about anything that's important."

"Yeah, that's just another reason you should go to therapy."

"You've got a therapist; therapy me," I say.

"Therapists have college degrees and Ph.D.s. I'm about to fail freshman bio," Claire says.

I wave her off. "It doesn't matter. Just ask me the questions your therapist asks you."

She huffs. "Okay. How're you feeling today?"

I shrug. "Fine."

"This isn't going to work if you're going to lie."

"I'm not lying! I feel fine."

"Says the girl screaming about how fine she is in a mall food court," Claire says. "Okay, we'll move on. Talk about what's bothering you."

"No. That's not what would happen next."

"How would you know?" Claire asks, raising her voice. "You've never been to therapy."

"It doesn't matter. I'm not answering that question," I say, pissed.

"Why not, Carly? Why won't you?" Claire pushes back.

"Because I feel rotten, okay?" I yell, slamming my hands on the table. Claire jumps. "I feel like shit. There are all these things I want, but I can't get them."

"Like what?"

"I don't know. How about Mollie? I really want to date her, but I can't date her because I fucked that up royally. Even if she forgives me she'll just find out that I'm not good enough and cheat on me like Emma did."

"Carly – "

"Oh," I say, holding up my hand. "I'm not finished yet. I can't even go to the college I want because that would require me to write something I didn't think was awful and let someone read it. And what if I do write something and I'm proud of it and I do let someone read it and they hate it? Like hate it more than *Twilight* and *Fifty Shades of Grey* combined. What then? What do I do then? I can't do the things I want because I'm terrified of not being good. That's why I coast. That's why I'm distant when it comes to people and the things that matter. I don't think I could survive not being good enough."

"Shit," Claire whispers.

"It's nothing," I say, wiping away a tear. "Come on, let's go before the mall cops throw us out of here."

"I feel like you should talk to somebody," Claire says, standing up with me.

"And I feel like I've just done enough talking for twenty years," I respond.

The car ride to Claire's is silent except for the radio quietly playing in the background. She reminds me where to turn, but doesn't try to continue our conversation. I'm thankful for that. Talking in general wears me out, but talking about my emotions makes me feel like the Nazi from the first Indiana Jones movie whose face melts off. Not that I'm a Nazi, I just get how it feels to have your face melt off. Emotionally, at least.

I drop Claire off and continue my drive home. Her stupid words keep playing over and over in my mind. There's this large part of me that's confident, but it's all surface. Surface is all I've got. Time and time again I've cried over things I'm afraid of because they matter. Like I played softball when I was younger and I was good. I know, get your gay jokes out now. I could've probably gone on to get a scholarship, but I gave up and told my parents my heart wasn't in it anymore. That was a total lie. My heart was in it, but before every practice or game, I would get really nervous and feel like I was going to throw up. What if I was no good? What if all the coaches were in on a joke and just pretending I was good? What if everyone laughed at me? Super healthy, right?

Well, since I'm allergic to talking about my feelings, I lied. I thought it was better to give up on something I loved than work through it. I'm sure my mom didn't believe me. She must've known it was deeper than that. In the end, it's fine. Softball wasn't my life the way writing is. If I was stuck on a desert island, I'd bring food, water, and an unlimited supply of pens and stationery. That's all I'd need.

With Oberlin, I feel like I'm paralyzed. On the one hand, it's my dream, within reach if I just write one stupid story. On the other hand, the thought of being rejected is beyond what I think I'm capable of handling. I could quit like I quit softball, but where would that get me? Dreamless, collegeless, probably working until I die at Spin Me, Baby.

I grunt in response to my parents' greetings as I sulk my way up to my room and flop face down on my bed. Maybe I can just dissolve into the duvet and never have to face anything ever again. I hear a knock at the door. So much for that.

"Carly? Can I come in?" my mom asks.

"If you must," I grumble. I feel the bed give a little as she sits down. Didn't this already happen today?

"You've been acting a little strange since last week. Is there something you want to talk about?" she asks as she lightly rubs my back.

What is it with people asking me to talk today? "No thanks, Mom."

"What about Oberlin? The deadline's coming up soon."

I sit up instantly. "How do you know about Oberlin?"

"You left the letter on your desk when you asked me to get your textbook the other day," she says.

"Oh," I say, shifting uncomfortably. "Are you mad?"

"Why would I be mad?" she asks.

"I mean, I hid it from you and Dad. Plus I don't think I want to do anything with science," I say sheepishly.

"Oh, honey. You don't have to go into science just because I went to school for science," my mom says. "I want you to be happy, and if going to Oberlin and being a writer is going to do that, then that's what I want for you."

"Really?" I ask.

"Of course! You're living your life, not mine," she says. "Is that what's been bothering you?"

I shrug. "One of many things."

"Well, let's fix this one first. I'm theorizing you're upset because you haven't written anything yet?"

"You're theorizing correctly," I say. I can feel the tears starting again.

"Okay, then write something," she says.

"Mom, that's like asking you to just find the cure for cancer," I say.

"You're always writing," she counters.

"How do you know what I'm always doing?"

"Your teachers have told me they've never seen a student take notes with such fervor before. Something tells me you aren't taking notes though."

"I mean, I'm definitely taking notes in calculus," I say, a little embarrassed.

"Well, you must be pretty good if Oberlin is considering you," she tells me.

The first tear hits my lip. "I don't know. All they've read are my hokey college essays. Which, honestly, they should've just burned before they read them. Would've saved everyone a lot of time. They were embarrassing."

"They made me laugh when I proofread them."

"You're my mom. You have to say that."

"I wouldn't lie to you. You're my daughter."

I snort. "That's exactly why you would lie to me."

"I have no trouble telling you the truth. I was the one who told you about Santa Claus, wasn't I?" she asks, lifting my chin. "Look, you're my kid. I want you to do what you want to do with your life. Oberlin and writing are what you want, right?"

I nod.

"So write! Use something you've already written and get it in before the deadline!"

"I can't!" I grumble. "I'm so nervous. I can't write anything that matters. What if they hate me?"

"Honey, you can't worry about that."

I sigh half-heartedly. "That's literally the only thing I can do."

"And what's that doing for you?" she asks. "I was like you. Worrying all the time. I took on the burden of being the only girl in my major in college. I worried constantly about how I could ruin everything for all the young girls in science if I failed. I cried to your grandmother all the time and I worried about every little thing I did. It was exhausting." She paused. "It's exhausting, right?"

"Yeah," I choke out.

"Your grandmother always said worrying was a waste

of time. It doesn't fix anything or protect anyone or make anything happen or not happen. It never has and it never will. She said it often enough that I finally came to believe it. All worrying does is make bright kids like you afraid to live their lives."

"You don't even know if I'm good or not."

"I know you're good and I know some part of you believes you're good," she says, wiping some of my tears away.

"Nope. I can't believe that."

She frowns. "I wish you would. Carly, you're smart, kind, and strong. I know you're a good writer. All you're missing is a bit of self-confidence. Once you start believing in yourself, even just a little bit, you're golden. It's all downhill from there. Pretty soon you'll be thinking you're the next Shakespeare."

I look up at her, tears still falling. "I don't know if I can do that. Besides, Shakespeare blows."

"Fine. You won't be the next Shakespeare; you'll be the first Allen. You can do it, Carly. Everyone around you knows that. It's time you start believing it yourself."

I take in a shaky breath. "Okay."

It's not okay, not totally, but for the first time I feel like it could be. Maybe I could be good at writing. Maybe I could write the next Great American Novel or, at the very least, be published by *The Atlantic*. This is wildly unstable ground and I'm still terrified, but the hurdles feel like they just got a little lower.

"Now," my mom says, shifting her position on the bed. "What else is going on?"

"Haven't I cried enough for one day, Mom?"

"You're on a roll. Might as well keep going," she says.

I shake my head. "It's nothing. Just girl troubles."

"Ah, so I'm the last person you want to talk to about this."

"I mean, I'd probably rather talk to you than Dad about it. He forgot Emma and I broke up, so he's not the best relationship-wise," I say, picking at the duvet cover.

"So, is that a yes to wanting to talk about it?" my mom asks quietly.

I shrug, and feel the waterworks starting up yet again.

"Look," she says. "I don't know anything about this girl or this situation, but I do know you, Carly."

"I screwed up bad."

"Badly," she says and I glare at her. "Few things can't be solved with a heartfelt apology and chocolate. Remember that, okay?"

"But what," I trail off and sigh. Talking is so hard. "What if this is one of those times when apologies and chocolates won't work?"

"Then you fight like hell, kiddo," my dad says from the doorway.

"How long have you been there?" I sniffle.

He shrugs and walks in. "Not long. It doesn't matter. I know a thing or two about love."

My mom kisses him and says, "He sure does."

Do they have to do that? "Gross."

"If you like this girl, fight for her. Give it your all. It's like Zac Efron says in *17 Again*."

"Oh my god," I groan. "Why are you like this?"

"'When you're young, everything feels like the end of the world, but it's not. It's just the beginning.'"

"Your dad's right," Mom says.

"No, Zac Efron's right," my dad says, shaking his head.

Mom seems to ignore that comment. "This feeling and your feelings about writing are interconnected. A little belief in yourself goes a long way."

Dad nods. "Fight like hell, then give up."

My mom smacks my dad on the chest. "Claude!"

"No, don't just give up. That's not what I said. I said fight like hell, *then* give up. Only after you've given it your absolute total all can you give in. I'm not talking about making a half-hearted effort and then calling it a day. I'm talking knock-down, drag-out, last breath, Hail Mary fighting. I know you've got it in you."

"I most certainly do not."

He shrugs. "You're my kid, you have to have it in you. You might not know it until you've got no other option.

You might even surprise yourself."

"We're going to get you posters to hang in your room that say Believe in Yourself and Fight Like Hell," my mom says, kissing my forehead. "Maybe if you see it every day, you'll start to believe it."

"You're gonna be fine, kiddo," my dad says, ruffling my hair. "Us Allens always get the girl."

They close the door behind them and I'm left at a crossroads. I could lie here and cry, let the Oberlin deadline pass, and let Mollie slip away. Or, I could do what Dad said and fight like hell. Right now I feel too weak to fight, but tomorrow is a new day. Tonight I'm going to cry a lot more and watch *The Notebook*.

I kind of hate this movie. The old people don't need to be in it at all. The whole hanging from the Ferris wheel thing is manipulative and Nicholas Sparks apparently hates the gays, but WHATEVER. I just like Ryan Gosling and everything he did to win back Rachel McAdams. He built her a house, for crying out loud. Find me someone on this planet who wouldn't want to marry house-building Ryan Gosling.

29

What About Me
by Moving Pictures

It's Sunday morning and I feel like I have an emotional hangover in place of the alcoholic one from Friday. All I could think about last night was Zoe and how she looked like someone had been kicking her dog repeatedly. Emma's probably moping like Zoe, and I guess I owe her an apology, even though this is exactly what she did to me. Whatever. I'm a bigger person. I can admit when I messed up.

I don't even want to think about the massive apology I need to give Mollie. My brain keeps reminding me that I really messed up poor, sweet, bystander Mollie Fae. That might be the worst part of all this. I sure as hell don't deserve her now, after what I've done. She should have somebody who writes songs for her and sings them, guitar in hand, under her window. Someone who's not an ass like me.

Hell. I'm going to suck up every ounce of pride I have

and apologize to Emma first. Out of all of the apologies I owe, that one should be the easiest. I pull on jeans and a white T-shirt and drive to her house like I have so many times before. I'm trying to come up with a speech in my head, but I've got nothing.

Only Emma's car is in the driveway, and that's a great sign. I can't imagine having to apologize while her family listens in. Somehow, Emma managed to spin the story of our break-up in her favor and come across as a victim. A+ for her, but now her family stares me down whenever they see me in public, despite the fact that Emma's the one who cheated on me. I ring the doorbell and a silhouette appears in the front door window. It swings open and there she is, looking perfectly fine, collected, and unaffected.

"Hi," I say, in a monotone.

She folds her arms. "Did you come here to screw up my family like you screwed up my relationship?"

"Well, I always did find your mom kind of cute," I say. This apology is going splendidly.

"Wow, okay. What do you want, Carly?"

"I came to apologize for the other night. It was a really shit thing to do and I'm sorry for everything."

"And?"

My eyebrows crease. "And what?"

"That's it? That's your entire apology?" she asks, leaning against the door frame.

I shrug. "I mean, yeah? I'm sorry, and if I had a time machine, I'd go back and not do it, but that can't happen. So I'm here, tail between my legs, telling you how sorry I am."

"I hope you know how well things were going with Zoe until you messed it all up."

"Hold on," I say, putting my hand up and losing the small amount of chill I have left. "You do realize this is why *we* broke up, right? We broke up because you went behind my back with Zoe."

"We didn't do anything until you and I broke up."

I snort. "Sure."

"Listen, if you're done, I have a relationship to fix," she says, and starts to close the door.

I can't help myself. "It looks like you're doing a terrible job at that since Zoe came into the store yesterday and bought a ton of break-up albums."

"Did you feel like shit knowing you're the reason she bought them? You're no better than Zoe was back when you and I were dating. You know that, right?"

"Stop it," I say, shaking my head.

"You don't get to act all high and mighty anymore because you did the exact same thing you've been hating me for." She smirks a little and I absolutely hate her. "How's that feel?"

"You know what?" I shout, walking across the porch to

stand right next to her. "I came over here to apologize and I was doing a damn good job of it, aside from that cute mom comment, but fuck you, Emma. Did I know you were still seeing Zoe? No. Do I feel terrible? Absolutely. A million times over, but not about you. No. You knew," I say, pointing a finger at her. "You had a girl waiting for you and you did it anyway. And I'm starting to get the feeling that Zoe didn't know you were taken all those months ago, but you knew then too. So, yeah, I made a bad decision for so many different reasons and there are people I need to apologize to for it, but I'm just now realizing you are not one of them."

"No one will trust you after this, Carly," she says, following me as I head down the stairs to the front sidewalk.

I turn around and laugh. "I've thought of myself as a really awful person for a long time, but I'm starting to see that I was wrong. It's you who's the awful girlfriend who can't keep it in her pants and doesn't care whose life she hurts. I'm done here."

Not my most eloquent speech, but I don't care. It's over now. Officially. Finally. I'm in my car and I see her still yelling from her porch. Emma is out of my life for good and I feel the weight of the world lessening.

The first real stop on the Towson-Wide Carly Allen Apology Tour is the record store. I see Scott in his office holding a record against each of his ears. What a loony. He sees me and gives me a nod, which I return. I pick up a copy of Ryan Adams' *Heartbreaker* and One Direction's *Take Me Home*. I walk back out to my car and pick up a notebook from the back seat. I'm writing Zoe a letter because I just can't face her after seeing Emma. Plus, prom's coming up and I'd prefer not to go in a cast. That is, if I even end up going to prom.

Dear Zoe,

I know I'm probably the last person you want to hear from, but I want to extend an olive branch. My name's Carly. For the better part of last year I was dating Emma. The same Emma you just found out was cheating on you. Small world, right? Anyway, I'm also the girl from the record store the other day, and coincidentally, the reason you and Emma broke up. Super duper small world. I'm so very sorry about all that. You have no reason to trust anything I say, but please believe I had no clue that the two of you were together. If I'd known, I never would've gone through with it. You have to believe me on this. I mean, I guess you don't really have to, but I'm hoping you will. Emma's the bad one in this scenario, and

I'm hoping you and I can come out of it as friends, or at least friendly. Moral of the story, I'm profoundly sorry you have to go through this and that I had a part in it.

In the bag you'll find two albums. One of them is Ryan Adams' *Heartbreaker* because it's the only quintessential breakup album you didn't buy the other day. The other's a One Direction album because things are going to get better and you're going to meet someone cute and sweet who won't cheat on you. The two of you will need something to sing along to. I'm really sorry we met this way and I hope you accept this apology.

All the best,
Carly

I slip the note inside the bag with the records and write Zoe's name on the front. She lives nearby. Last summer, Emma would spend all her time there while I worked at the store. I don't know how Emma swung it so the two of us never met in all that time, and I wonder what she'd think about me going over there now.

I recognize the house instantly and pull over in front of it. I wonder which room's hers and if she's sitting up there now crying over *Stay with Me* by Sam Smith. That's what I'd be doing.

As I climb out of the car, I decide to leave it running so I can make a quick escape. I walk up to the door, put the package on the porch, ring the doorbell, sprint back to my car, and throw it into drive. By the time I'm three houses away, I see Zoe open the door. She looks just as ragged as she did yesterday at the record store. Poor kid. Neither one of us deserves this. I know that now.

30

Bad Moon Rising
by Creedence Clearwater Revival

On Monday morning, I show up late to class for the first time in my high school career. I'm hungover from the whiskey I stole from my parents' basement stash. Annie stares at me, wide-eyed, and I'm sure I look dismal. I'm wearing the same white t-shirt and jeans from yesterday. There are coffee stains on my shirt and I don't care.

I barely register Mr. Hall's comment about my being late and how my parents will be called. There's nothing to do but slump in my seat, arms crossed, with a scowl on my face. I can barely stay awake. Last night, I was up way past two a.m. looking at Mollie Fae's Facebook page. Like hardcore heavy stalking.

I miss her.

It occurred to me to message her, and the taunting green circle next to her name stayed lit until I passed out. I probably wrote at least thirty messages that I never sent. They ranged from as short as "I'm sorry" to as long as the last Harry Potter book. None of it will ever see the light of day. The messages weren't right; there was something missing. Also, I'm not about to try to win a girl back over Facebook. That seems desperate.

The bell rings and I slowly make my way out the door. Out of nowhere, someone pushes me into the girls' bathroom.

"What the hell?"

"I could ask you the exact same thing, Carly," Annie says, crossing her arms.

"Ugh, Annie. I am not in the mood for this," I say.

"Yeah, well, my best friend smells like a distillery and looks like shit. You haven't worn a wrinkled t-shirt to school since sophomore year," Annie says, poking me in the stomach.

"Ouch!" I yell.

"You also haven't responded to a single text all weekend. What happened?"

I sigh. "I slept with Emma."

"*Emma* Emma? The girl who cheated on you Emma?" Annie's incredulous.

I nod and feel a few tears trying to escape from behind my eyelids.

"Oh, honey. Come here," Annie says, pulling me into a hug.

"It was so, so stupid," I sob. "I was just so drunk and

Mollie wasn't there."

"Yeah, that probably wasn't your finest hour," Annie says.

"That's not helping," I say.

Annie pulls back. "Well, it's not really that big a deal, right? Mollie wasn't there, so she doesn't know."

"She kissed me the next morning."

"I leave you alone for one weekend and your life becomes an episode of *Gossip Girl*. What's college going to be like for you?" Annie asks.

"She kissed me and then she saw Emma." I gesture kind of wildly.

"Yeah, I know how sex works, Carly," Annie says, blushing slightly.

I look at her funny. "Wait, did you and Todd?"

She blushes. "Now's not the time to talk about that. We need to figure out what you're going to do."

The warning bell rings. "Go to class," I say.

"I don't like seeing you like this." Annie hesitates.

"Well, until I figure out what to do, this is me," I say, wiping my face on my shoulder.

I walk into the hallway and I'm hit like a tsunami by the sight of Mollie Fae. She's talking to Madison, who sees me first. Mollie follows her gaze and looks right at me. I feel like a deer caught in headlights, upstream without a paddle. Like I'm in my underwear in front of the entire school. Like a fool. Plain and simple.

Mollie looks at me for a long moment and I'm trying hard to get my mouth to say something. To say her name or just a simple sorry. Almost anything would be good. Hell, I'd take even a caveman-like grunt at this point.

Madison narrows her eyes and throws her arm around Mollie, guiding her toward their classroom. I watch them disappear, praying Mollie will turn around and look at me. Just one look over her shoulder that tells me winning her back isn't a fool's errand.

I'm about to give up. Annie's trying to get me to go to class, but I won't leave until Mollie's 100% around that corner. Completely out of sight. Out of sight, but never out of mind.

It's a blink and you miss it moment. If we were in a movie, it would've gotten the slow motion, close-up treatment. As they're rounding the corner, Mollie's head turns. For the briefest of moments, our eyes meet. It's almost enough to make me chase after her. It's hope. There's a chance in hell, however improbable. It's not enough to make things right and I still feel like I'm on a downward spiral, but think I'm finally close to the bottom.

31

Bad Reputation
by Joan Jett & the Blackhearts

Every school has a resident senior who won't graduate. Sometimes that senior's just too good at sports and wants one more jewel in a *Glory Days* crown. Sometimes that kid can't pass algebra and no one seems to care. Whatever the reason, the fifth year seems to be the perfect origin story for bullies.

Our resident sexist, bullying, fifth-year senior is Steve Underwood, the quarterback who's been leading our team to mediocrity since his sophomore year. He's consistently ensured that the team never places better than eighth in the county. What a fine accomplishment.

Until the second half of his second senior year, Steve was relatively harmless. He'd make stupid jokes in class, but there was nothing rude about them. Just dumb fart jokes. He drew dicks in textbooks, which isn't bad, just weird. I have no clue why guys love penises so much. That's not even a me being a lesbian thing. It's a genuine thing I don't understand. Girls don't draw vaginas everywhere. Guys are so concerned that a gay dude might look at them in the locker room, but they've tagged every surface imaginable with dicks. Makes no sense.

Things changed after Christmas break. Maybe it's because he's finally going to graduate this year, or because his girlfriend broke up with him. Who knows. Steve came back in January ready to ruin lives. He flushes freshmen in the toilet and gives them wedgies because he's not creative enough to think of anything else.

Today he's making a scene in the cafeteria, yelling at kids from his table of fools. I can hear him from the other end of the room, whistling at freshman girls who walk by the table. It makes me want to punch him in the face.

For about five minutes, I'm able to tune him out and focus on my table. Todd and Annie are talking about prom and matching colors. The kids in the band are planning a set list for Cameron's party. Claire's here too. She's supposed to be going over bio notes, but she's been quiet for a while. I let my eyes drift over to Mollie's table. She's in her usual spot between Madison and Amber from government. My stomach feels weird.

I remember I have to look over Claire's work before lunch ends, but she's gone. Her papers are still spread out on the table, but her seat's empty. I look around the cafeteria and see her standing next to Steve Underwood, telling him to leave everyone alone. I smile a little for the first time today. She's totally hard-headed and it's pretty much guaranteed that he won't stop being a jerk, but I'm glad her heart's in the right place.

I guess Claire gets the message that nothing's going to change because she starts to walk away from the fools' table. As she does, Steve flicks up her skirt and smacks her ass in front of the entire school. I'm running toward them before I even realize it.

"Hey, Steve!" I yell. Claire looks over at me, her usually strong face now embarrassed and teary.

Steve laughs and turns around. "Oh, look at this. Carly Allen. Here to save the day."

"Someone's got to when the quarterback's a total ass," I say.

He flips me off. "Get out of here. Nothing's wrong. This pretty girl and me were just talking." He moves to touch Claire and she smacks his hand away.

"Don't touch me," she says, her voice angry and shaky at the same time.

"Leave her alone, Steve," I say, moving closer.

"You're two feet tall," he says, laughing. "Bring it on, elf."

By this time, there's a hush over the cafeteria. People don't care about their lunches or next period's unfinished homework. They're paying attention to me and Steve and whatever's going to happen between us. I feel my muscles tense and I want to hit him. I want him to know he can't just touch any girl he wants. I want him to know he's being a jerk and that's not okay. I want to hit him for making Claire feel like this.

Maybe it's because of the terrible thing that's happened to Mollie and me, but I feel like I have nothing to lose. That could be what had me running down the aisle toward Steve before I could even process what was happening. Am I trying to show her that even though I did a terrible thing, I can still care about people? I don't know.

Steve laughs sharply. "Ha! I knew you wouldn't do anything."

I've never punched anyone before. All I know is that you're not supposed to tuck your thumb into your hand because it'll break or something. That's the only fully formed thought racing through my head when my fist connects with Steve Underwood's jaw. It hurts. Thumb or no thumb. I feel like every bone in my hand is shattered. I must've done something right, though, because Steve's lying on the floor howling.

Teachers are swarming around us, pulling me back in case I want to punch him again. I don't want to punch him again. I barely wanted to punch him the first time, but I'm glad I did. Somebody had to put him in his place. I don't care that violence is wrong. Knocking the mediocre high school football star to the ground with one punch is pretty dope. Thank you, Jane Fonda workout tapes.

The new freshman social studies teacher is guiding me away from Steve. We pass Claire and she manages to give me a hug. It throws me for a loop and my arms stay limp by my side for a moment until my brain finally catches up. I hug her back until the social studies teacher says it's time to go to the principal's office.

Claire's eyes are red and a little puffy. I know we'll never speak of this again. If I do attempt to bring it up, she'll say she doesn't remember or she wasn't crying or she'll just flat out ignore me. And that'll be okay.

We walk through the rows and rows of tables categorized by clique. When we pass the stoner skaters, one of them stands and starts a slow clap. His friends join in, and then it spreads to the art kids and the band kids and the geeks. Even the English nerds put down their books. Every kid in the cafeteria is clapping except for bloody-nosed, black-eyed Steve Underwood and his band of fools. The cafeteria is roaring and teachers are looking nervous, like this could all get out of control.

Who knew punching the resident bully could unify a school so fast?

32

Stand By Me
by Ben King

"Now, Carly," Principal Davis says, looking away from her computer screen, "there's nothing in your file that would lead me to believe you would do something like this."

"There's nothing in there about how much I hate misogynistic jerks? Weird."

"Do you know how much trouble you could be in? Suspended from school, kicked out of the tutoring program, class speaker privileges revoked," Principal Davis says. "Summer school."

"I won class speaker?" I ask, excitement bubbling. Then I remember why I'm here. "Sorry."

"Sorry for what? For punching Steve or for calling him a misogynistic jerk?" she asks.

Neither, my heart says. "I don't know."

"You don't feel sorry?"

"He was harassing Claire. What was I supposed to do?

He smacked her butt in front of the whole school!"

"And that allows you to just punch him? We use our words here, Ms. Allen."

"Something tells me words aren't going to change Steve Underwood. Not after all these years."

Principal Davis takes a deep breath and puts her glasses on the desk. "Violence is never the answer." I roll my eyes.

"I need you to be serious," she says sternly.

"Look, I'd really like to not be suspended. So I'll just apologize to whoever I have to apologize to."

"Do you believe he deserved what you did to him?"

"Do you?" I ask.

"I wasn't there."

"I was," I say, sitting up straighter in my chair. "I'd like my file to note that I did try to talk to Steve before I punched him. It didn't work. But I'm not sorry for standing up for Claire. I know I should regret punching another person, but I can't bring myself to feel bad for Steve Underwood. He was bullying Claire."

Just then, Claire bursts through the door.

"Principal Davis, you can't suspend Carly!" she gasps.

"As principal, I may do whatever I please. This is a private meeting, so I'm going to have to ask you to leave," Principal Davis says sternly.

"Here," Claire says, pushing two pieces of paper across the desk. "The first one is a quiz from the beginning of the year. The other is one after Carly started tutoring me this semester. My grade went from a D+ to an A-."

I look over at her. "A-? Nice job."

"See," she says, gesturing toward me. "Carly cares about me. She's why I'm not going to be held back. If you kick her out of the tutoring program, I will fail."

Principal Davis hesitates. "Her skill as a tutor does not diminish the fact that she knocked a boy to the ground."

"Yeah," Claire says. "A boy who flipped my skirt up and squeezed my ass. A boy who wouldn't leave me alone. That's the boy you want to protect? Are you going to say next that it was my fault because I was wearing a skirt? He's the one you should be suspending!"

"She's got a point," I say.

Principal Davis stares at us. "Mr. Underwood's punishment is none of your concern."

"Steve's getting punished? So Carly goes free?" Claire asks.

"Not so fast," she says. "Carly, while Steve may have been acting inappropriately, that's not an excuse to haul off and punch him." I nod and she continues. "That being said, this is also your first infraction. I think a week of after-school detention is fair."

"Sounds reasonable," Claire says.

"What are you? My lawyer?" I ask Claire.

"You will also use this as a teaching opportunity for

Claire and the rest of Ms. Bennett's class," Principal Davis continues. "Teach them something."

"Roger that," I say.

Principal Davis dismisses us and tells me to go to the nurse and get some ice for my now terribly bruised and swollen knuckles. Everyone else is in class, so it's just us walking through the quiet hallways.

"So, uh, thanks for that back there," I say, looking over at her.

"Do not get sad on me," she says, shaking her head. "I'm serious."

"Yeah, I'm serious, too. It wasn't going too well before you came in. I was just so angry that Steve was going to get out of it without even a slap on the wrist."

"That saying doesn't make sense."

I laugh. "No old timey sayings make sense."

It's quiet again. Just the sound of Claire's flip-flops slapping against the tile floor and my boots scuffing along. I try to flex my bruised hand and grimace. How do people go around punching other people all willy-nilly and act as if it doesn't hurt? Of all the lies Hollywood has told me, I think this may be the worst.

"Thank you," Claire says quietly.

I throw my arm around her shoulders and pull her close. I don't think there's anything more that needs to be said.

33

Just Another Girl
by The Killers

When I get home from my first after-school detention, I walk into my room and find Annie lying on the bed, reading my copy of *Tuck Everlasting*. She sits up when I drop my backpack on the floor and slouch into the chair at my desk.

"Hey."

"Hey," I say back.

"I'm sorry," we both say at the same time. Then we both smile.

"I'm sorry I was an ass this morning and I'm sorry I didn't answer any of your texts all weekend."

"I'm sorry your life has become a full-on CW TV show," Annie says, and I laugh.

"Yeah, I kind of wish that hadn't happened."

"So how are you going to win Mollie back?"

"Now you sound like my father," I say.

"Clearly you aren't over her."

I shrug. "Clearly."

"So what's your plan? The Carly I know wouldn't give up," she says.

"That Carly doesn't exist. It's all fake. Claire therapisted me."

"Real confidence, false confidence. No one can tell," Annie says. "Especially when you sing. I know!" she says, all excited. "Write her a song! You're still playing at Cameron's End of Year Extravaganza, right?"

"As far as I know."

"This is perfect!" Annie exclaims. "Write that girl a song."

I have written her a song. I wrote it at work after Zoe came into the store and after I vomited the first time. There's a rough melody to go along with it and I made a demo of it on GarageBand at two o'clock Saturday morning.

It doesn't feel like I have much to lose anymore. The Carly Allen from two weeks ago would have sat through every Kidz Bop album rather than consider letting someone hear a song she'd written. A kind of bottom of the barrel feeling has taken over me and consequences don't seem to matter much anymore. Which, in a weird sort of way, is actually improving my confidence. It's like, how much worse could things get?

I walk over to my backpack and pull out a notebook

covered in pictures and news clippings. There are papers peeking out of the pages and I pull out the one I wrote the song on.

I cough. "This is really embarrassing, so be gentle with me. I wrote this. I'm sure it's terrible and probably needs a lot of work, but it's a song."

"Can I see it?" she asks.

"Yeah, just don't read it out loud, and if it's the worst thing you've ever read just say peanut butter. It'll be our code word so we won't have to talk about it if it's bad."

"Carly," she starts.

"No," I interrupt. "That's the only condition."

"Fine," she says, and I hand over the paper.

This is a terrible plan. I pace back and forth as Annie reads. Super slowly, I might add. I could've gone to Mollie's house and won her over by now. It's like she's reading every single pencil scratch on the page. I've bitten my nails down to nothing and I'm not even a nail biter.

Annie clears her throat. "Wow."

I whip around to face her. "Like peanut butter wow or good wow?"

"Good wow," she says, looking over the words. "Really good wow."

The weight on my shoulders dissipates a little. "Really?"

"Yeah. Do you have music to go along with it?"

"I've got a GarageBand file I made when I was drunk,

225

but that's it. Mark and Matt are good at that stuff," I say.

"You should show it to them. I think this could really work." Annie grins at me.

I grab the paper out of her hand. "Shoot. I forgot I have band practice!" I throw my laptop and notebook into a backpack, then turn to look at Annie. "Thank you."

She pulls me into a hug. "I love you, Carly Allen."

"I love you, too," I say, and hug her tighter.

"Come on, I'll walk out with you," she says.

"Were you planning on staying here while I was gone?" I joke.

"What do you think I was doing before you got here? Plus, your dad and I are pals. I'm beating him at Words with Friends," Annie says.

"You're playing Words with Friends with my dad?" I ask.

She nods. "And your mom and your grandmother on your mom's side. They're pretty good."

I laugh as I lock the door and buckle my bike helmet. "Sometimes I forget you're not my sister."

"If I was your sister, I'd have an easier time beating some sense into you," Annie says. "I had to break into your house today so you couldn't avoid me."

"Wait a second," I say, stopping in the middle of the sidewalk. "How did you get into my house?"

"Don't worry about it," she laughs, then gets into her

car and drives away with a wave.

****

"Hi, everybody," I say as I ride my bike into Bryan's garage. The band's all there. "Sorry I'm late."

"We were worried something happened to you," Matt says.

Bryan scoffs.

"Some of us were," Heather adds.

"Sorry. I had detention." I prop my bike against the wall.

"Oh, yeah. I forgot you knocked Steve Underwood to the ground," Bryan says, holding up a hand for a high-five.

"No thank you." I leave him hanging.

"That was really cool," Mark says.

"It was really stupid. My hand hurts like hell," I say, showing them my blue-green knuckles.

"Nasty," Matt says.

"I was also late because I wrote a song." I avoid eye contact with everyone and pull my laptop out of my backpack.

"You did?" Heather asks.

"Yeah. I was thinking we could try to have it ready for Cameron's party."

"That's soon. We'd have like a week and a half," Bryan says.

"I know, but, I really, really need it ready for that night."

"Why?" Matt asks.

"She wants to bang that girl," Bryan says.

"Emma?" Mark asks.

"No!" I say. "Mollie. I'm not banging her and I'm not talking about it with any of you. All you need to know is I messed up and I need you to help me fix it."

"Let's hear it," Heather says.

"Okay," I say, plugging my laptop into the amp. "It's really rough, so keep an open mind. I think the twins will need to help it a lot. Oh, and the tempo is off and I don't really understand GarageBand."

"Just play the damn song," Bryan says.

I watch their faces during the song. Bryan's impossible to read. Heather has a small smile on her face and is drumming a beat along with the song. The twins are nodding their heads and whispering to each other. How do musicians do this on a regular basis? Mercifully, it's finally over.

"So?"

"It's really good," Heather says. "I like the lyrics."

"Lyrics are great," Mark says. "The music's a little funky and I think the key should be changed, but it's got great bones."

Matt nods his head. "Great bones."

"Good enough bones to be a fleshed-out song in time for the extravaganza?" I ask.

Heather shakes her head. "Don't say fleshed."

"Definitely doable," Mark says.

I give a sigh of relief. "Bryan? What did you think?"

He looks over at me. "Carly, if you have enough balls to play that song at this party, I will streak at your graduation."

"Bullshit," I say.

"Guarantee it. We all will," Bryan says, gesturing at the rest of the band.

Matt starts vehemently shaking his head. "Not me."

Bryan shushes him. "Solidarity. She's putting her heart on the line and you're nervous about letting your pasty ass get some sun?"

I stare at them, shocked. "Guys, you don't have to streak at graduation. And I don't know if this song is ready to play at the party. You heard the twins."

Mark pipes up. "It's a good song, Carly. Really good. She's gonna love it."

"I think we should streak," Heather says.

Our heads whip around in her direction and we ask in unison, "You *do?*"

She shrugs. "I've never streaked before. It's on my bucket list, so I might as well do it when I'm young."

"This is going better than I imagined," Bryan says. "I

thought Heather would be the hardest to convince. Man up, twins."

"I resent that statement, which implies that it's masculine to want to do something bold," Heather complains.

"Not now," Bryan says.

"Woman up," Heather says. "The three of you." She points to me and the twins.

"What do I have to woman up about?" I ask.

"You're going to pansy out on the song," Bryan says. "You're already making excuses about how it's not done when it is. It's a great song. Hell, I'd date you if you wrote that song about me and then sang it to me in front of the whole school."

"Yeah, but it's gotta be good enough to win the girl back," I say.

"It is," Mark says, then pauses for a moment. "I'm gonna streak."

"Mark!" Matt exclaims.

"Yes! One more to go!" Bryan says cheerfully.

"I'm doing this for Carly," Mark says, and I'm touched. "If you want to get the girl, this song will do it."

"Fine," I say bravely. "I'll do it if Matt streaks."

"You can't put that on me! This is like sexual harassment," Matt whines.

"No it's not," Bryan says. "You'll just have to live with

the guilt for the rest of your life, knowing you're the reason Carly and Mollie aren't married."

"Whoa," I say. "Marriage is a little much."

"I'm exaggerating to guilt this kid into taking his clothes off," Bryan says, rolling his eyes. "Don't you want to tell your children the story of how you streaked at your bandmate's graduation?"

"Not really, but I see your point," Matt says. "I'll do it, but Carly, you'd better kiss her. Kiss her for all of us."

I give him a weird look. "You had me until the end, but I guess your heart's in the right place."

"It's decided then," Heather says, playing a rim shot.

"We're really doing this?" I ask.

"What've we got to lose?" Bryan responds.

He's right. I have nothing left to lose. If Mollie hates this song, or if we crash and burn, it'll be no worse than my life right now. In fact, it might even be better because at least then I'll know if we have a chance. Eventually, things will be okay. I might be happy or I might cry for a while, but I'll have an answer. I'm going to college in four months. Do I really want to leave Mollie behind not knowing? No. I'm not jetting off to college without an answer.

"Absolutely nothing."

34

Can't Fight This Feeling
by REO Speedwagon

The past week and a half has been an utter blur. School all day, detention, band practice until ten. Then wake up and do it all over again. The twins say we're ready and the song is sonically cohesive, whatever that means. There was a part of me that didn't want this to work. A part that kept hoping a reason would pop up to cancel the show, but tonight's the night and we're here setting up.

"Hey, do you need anything before I go?" Cameron asks. He's been hanging out with us, but now it's time for him to do whatever he needs to do to get things set up inside.

I wipe my hands and stand up, taking a break from the amp I've been fiddling with. "No thanks. I think we're pretty good."

"Yeah, some alcohol," Bryan says.

Cameron nods and walks back toward his house. We're setting up in the pool house because the bedroom's got these big sliding doors that open up to the backyard. With our minimal knowledge of acoustics, we assume that by being at least partially inside, some of the noise will be contained. All the furniture is pushed against the back wall, making the rest of the space virtually inaccessible.

It's hard not to remember the last time I was in this house. It was months ago, when Mollie and I officially met again. There was so much potential that night, and I'd be lying if I said I hadn't thought I'd be at this party with her. I would've shown her how to get on the roof and we could've sat up there, all alone, watching the stars. Or something. Doesn't matter anymore, does it?

Here I am, though. On time to a party for the first time ever, about to play a real, live gig.

****

"This is stupid. We should just bail. No one's gonna like us," Heather moans as she hyperventilates.

"Chill," Bryan says. "We'll be fine."

"What on earth are you basing that on?" Matt asks, pacing.

Bryan shrugs. "That Claire girl who follows Carly around."

"I'm tutoring her," I say.

"Whatever. She makes me think of that grumpy girl from *Parks and Rec* who likes nothing, but she liked us when she heard us."

"He's right," I say. "We'll be fine. Everyone's drunk, so they won't even be listening."

"You're very calm for someone who's trying to win over a girl." Mark grins at me.

"Yeah, trying not to think about that yet," I say, wiping my sweaty palms on my pants. "It's the last song on the set list. I can't freak out yet."

Cameron pokes his head through the door. "You guys ready? People are getting a little rowdy out here."

"They want to hear us?" Heather asks.

"Are you kidding? You're the talk of the party," Cameron says. "Don't screw up."

"Holy shit." Matt watches Cameron leave.

"Come here, guys. Group huddle," I say.

"No. Not doing that." Bryan tries to squirm away, but Heather pulls him in.

"It's just like we're playing in Bryan's garage, okay? That's it," I say.

"Not entirely true," Mark says.

"Come on, Mark. Work with me. We're all going to do a shot of that whiskey I see behind Heather's head and then we're going put on a damn good show."

"Yeah!" Matt exclaims.

After we all down a shot of whiskey (which some of us handle better than others), everyone grabs their instruments and we line up by the door. Heather's first. We're starting off with *Hello* by Martin Solveig and Dragonette. Yes, you do know this song. It's the one used in that tennis music video that got really popular a few years ago. For some reason it stayed popular at our school. The twins cut it down a lot and added their own orchestrations, so now it's more of an intro to the next song rather than a song on its own. I don't need to justify this to you, just know it sounds cool.

Heather leads us out and the lights go on as she starts the beat. The twins go next, plug in their guitars, and play that first chord. The crowd's getting louder and louder. Bryan goes, and then it's just me. I'm terrified and I feel like I've forgotten the words to every song on the set list. I jump a little to get some of the nerves out.

My cue comes and I'm thankful my feet remember to move when they're supposed to. Once I'm on that makeshift stage, though, all the nerves are gone. Song goes into song, and before I know it we're at the end of the list. Now or never.

"Are you having a good time out there?" I ask, twirling the microphone cord around my finger. That's greeted with cheers, hollers, and whistles. I laugh. "Good, good. How would you feel if we finished up with an original song? One we wrote." Cheers again. "Cool. That's what I was hoping to hear."

"Carly told you we wrote this song," Bryan says into his mic, "but she wrote it. None of us are as weepy and dramatic as she is."

"Bryan's not wrong. Yeah, this is a song I wrote. It's about a girl." There are some wolf whistles, but I ignore them. "This is a song I wrote about a girl who I hope is here tonight. It's about how I messed up really badly. I'm talking monumentally. This is my apology to her. I, uh, I just hope she's here to hear it." My voice trails off and I'm scanning every face in the crowd, but Mollie's isn't one of them. My shoulders drop just a little. "This is also about Ryan Gosling because he always gets the girl. Even when he messes up. I'd really like to be the Ryan Gosling in this story."

There are some cheers, and I look again for Mollie. I assume she's here somewhere. Pretty much everyone from our senior class is here. Even kids who don't usually get invited are here. This is *the* party to end all high school parties, so she has to be here. She said she was coming, but that was when things weren't so dark and gloomy.

If she's not here, I can't blame her. If I was in her shoes, I don't know if I'd be here. I guess I'm not surprised, it just sucks. How can I fight for her if she's not even here to fight for?

"Hey! You done soliloquizing, yet?" Bryan yells. I'm jolted back to the here and now.

236

I swallow hard. "Yeah. Let's do this. Grab your girl, grab your guy, if you're lucky enough to have one. If not, fall in love with the person next to you. This song's called *Ryan*. We hope you like it."

> This is my Hail Mary
> My I wrote you every day for a year
> Pouring down rain, *Notebook* moment
> I'm no Elton John, my song is barely a gift
> But I swear I could be your Ryan Gosling
> If you'd just give me a chance
>
> If I could, I'd be 18 forever
> You next to me 'til the end of time
> Hair pretty and wild, tarot cards all around
> You're the queen of hearts in my deck
> And I'm nothing but a fool
> A hanged man, entirely hung up on you
> So cut my rope and set me free
> Oh, darling, won't you run away with me?
>
> I'd put my last quarter in a pay phone
> So I could hear your voice again
> A hundred dollars of gas in my tank
> If it meant seeing you at the end
> There's not much I wouldn't do

And there's a hell of a lot in my way
But, god, I'm not giving up this fight
Cause honey, you're my baby
And I'm praying you're in my corner tonight

If I could, I'd be 18 forever
You next to me 'til the end of time
Hair pretty and wild, tarot cards all around
You're the queen of hearts in my deck
And I'm nothing but a fool
A hanged man, entirely hung up on you
So cut my rope and set me free
Oh, darling, won't you run away with me?

They say you might've moved on
And that's a real damn pity
I know I'm unqualified and way out of line
But I really think you should pick me
Lemme be your girl
Mama didn't raise no James Marsden
Baby, I was born to be a Gosling

If I could, I'd be 18 forever
You next to me 'til the end of time
Hair pretty and wild, tarot cards all around
You're the queen of hearts in my deck

And I'm nothing but a fool
A hanged man, entirely hung up on you
So cut my rope and set me free
And run
Oh, come on girl
Just run away with me

As soon as the song ends, the party goes nuts. People are cheering and chanting for us to play it again. I barely register any of it because I finally see Mollie Fae. My dad's words echo in my head.

Knock-down, drag-out.

I drop the microphone and it screeches, but I'm too busy fighting through the crowd to care. Mollie's at the very back and people are trying to push me onto the stage to sing another song. I will. I'll sing another song. I promise I'll sing songs until the sun comes up, but only after I fix this.

Mollie watches me getting closer to her, and I can see tears in her eyes. She starts to slowly back away and (it's possible I'm projecting here) she looks conflicted. It's as if she wants to stay, but there's another part of her telling her to run. Luck doesn't seem to be with me because she's jogging through the house by the time I break out of the crowd.

I jump over couches and people and stumble out the

front door, desperate to find her. She's at her car, hand on the door, trying to get the key in.

"Mollie! Hey, Mollie, stop!" I cry, running over to her.

"I can't," she says, her voice breaking as she opens the door and turns to look at me.

I stop dead in my tracks, about twenty feet away from her. She's crying and looks like she's been through hell. Her dress is wrinkled and we have matching bags under our eyes. She stares at me for so long I wonder if she's having her own internal debate, like the one I had when she asked me if I liked her after she kissed me. She could run to me. She could forgive me. She could drive away now and never think of me again.

Mollie shakes her head. "I can't. Not yet. I'm so sorry," she says, and gets into the car.

The beat-up Beetle sputters to life and she drives away. Just like that. I walk into the middle of the sleepy suburban road and watch as the car comes to a full and complete stop at the end of the neighborhood because of course, even now, she obeys the traffic laws. Then the right turn signal blinks on and she's gone.

Yes, I know what you're thinking. "Carly, you didn't fight for her. You just let her go. Why didn't you try to stop her?" And maybe you're right. I could've run to her car and grabbed the door before she closed it. I could've dramatically jumped in front of the car so she'd have to stop and listen to me. But I didn't. Why? I get that you're supposed to fight for someone until you're beaten and down and finished, but maybe she doesn't want that.

I just don't know.

35

*Livin' On A Prayer
by Bon Jovi*

My Sunday has been uneventful. I opened Spin Me, Baby and drank coffee until it was time to go home. The morning seemed to just happen all around me while I watched from a distance. If you tell me it was all just a hallucination, I might believe you. It felt like I was watching my life from the other side of a window. Last night threw me into neutral just as my engine was revving, and I have no idea how to get back in the race, or even where the finish line is.

After my shift at the store, I came home to my parents celebrating the fact that I got into the Oberlin Creative Writing program. Apparently, the letter came yesterday, but our neighbors, the Jacksons, got it in their mail. I feel like the wind has been knocked out of me. I did it. I got into Oberlin. It doesn't feel real and I'm not sure I truly believe it, even as I read the letter I'm holding in my hands. There's the pop of a champagne bottle and I feel the light spray fall onto my hair.

I'm going to Oberlin.

I'm going to Oberlin, writing scholarship and all. There's a big, stupid grin on my face. I overnighted the story, just before the deadline. I wrote it after listening to the mixtape Mollie made for me. It won't be the next Great American Novel, but it doesn't have to be. It's a story about coming of age. Write what you know, y'know? And no, it's not this story. I don't know why I'm writing all this down. Maybe for my kids or posterity or something. Or maybe I like *The Notebook* a lot more than I let on. The point is, come August, I will be a creative writing major at Oberlin. When will it sink in?

After the initial excitement, the evening marches on as usual. My mom tells a story over dinner that ends with a centrifuge being the punch line. It makes my dad cry with laughter, but I barely hear any of it. I can't help thinking about what it means that I got into Oberlin. People read words I wrote and thought I put them in a good order. That's all writing is. Am I technically a writer now? What am I going to worry about now that I'm accepted? I feel like I'm having an identity crisis. Writing's this thing I love so much and it was something I was terrified of losing. But I didn't lose it. Even if I didn't get in, I don't think I would've lost it. It's a part of me. Are some things impossible to lose?

This is turning my world inside out.

I think my parents think I'm overwhelmed about Oberlin and graduation and growing up and everything, so they let me skip out on family movie night. I'm ecstatic about that because it's Dad's turn to pick and he got *Charlie St. Cloud*. Why can't Zac Efron make good movies so I don't have to suffer? (I'm not including *High School Musical* in that statement because that's true cinematic art. Wildcats forever.)

High school isn't over yet, so I sit down at my desk and pull out my physics homework. It's the last shred of high school that remains. In lieu of a final, the teacher gave us a packet of problems that covers the entire year and let us work on it at home for two weeks. Of course, I've barely started on it because any semblance of normalcy hit the fan two weeks ago and I've been in a tailspin ever since.

The first question is about potential energy. It's from the beginning of the semester, which means I have no clue how to answer it. Let's see, there's a box that weighs something and it's on a shelf with some joules of potential energy, so how high is the box? How about I don't give a shit meters high. I drop my pencil onto the desk and walk over to my record collection.

Because I love my records more than I love my future children, my vinyl collection is in pristine condition. It's organized by genre, then alphabetized by last name or band name, just like Mollie Fae's. I'm a big, big fan of '80s hair bands. The world was so Technicolor and neon, you couldn't help but fall in love through the haze of hairspray. I've got Pat Benatar, Cheap Trick, Joan Jett, Foreigner, Cyndi Lauper because yes, *She's So Unusual* is one of the greatest albums in the world. I decide on *No Protection* by Starship.

I go back and look at the physics problems, twirling my pencil as I flip through my notebook, trying to find the formula for potential energy. I think it's near the gravity stuff, but I can't find it. This stupid formula's written down somewhere, but where? Why didn't I take better notes?

As I go through the notebook, I see a Post-it note folded and stuck on the top of one of the pages. It's Mollie Fae's handwriting, and my stomach does a couple of flips. It's just some formulas, chicken scratch from the day we studied together. Completely nonsensical. My fingers are tracing the little letters. Terrible penmanship, but I think it's the cutest. I smile and forget about the physics homework. I avoid it a little longer. Forget the actual formula – this is real potential energy.

The second track begins and the opening drum beat of *Nothing's Gonna Stop Us Now* crackles through my speakers. I can't help but sing along softly at first. You can say a lot about '80s songs being cheesy, but all songs are cheesy. Every single song that's ever been written is cheesy as hell.

But every single song is magical and can change the whole entire world. I've listened to this song a thousand times, but tonight it's like I'm hearing the words for the first time. I'm overcome by the twinkling piano and stadium guitar chords. Finally, something louder than the inhibitions and doubts in my mind. I'm on my bed belting it out now, carried away by the magic of '80s power ballads. My empty bedroom is getting the performance of a lifetime. The song ends and I'm kneeling on the floor after a dramatic power slide. My chest is heaving, but I don't feel tired. I feel unstoppable. Unyielding. Nothing's gonna stop me now.

For a while, I'd started to believe this was all pointless, that there was no way I was going to have a true fairy tale romance. Well, to hell with all those people who say fairy tales aren't real and love is just a lot of work. No shit. I know it's a lot of work, but it's also going to be every bit as magical as I've been led to believe. Life has to be full of fairy tales and dragons and knights with really good hair because I have really good hair and it shouldn't go to waste just because I got a little lost along the way.

All I want in this lifetime is to feel the way '80s music feels. Yes, cheesy, but unbroken, invincible, young forever, regardless of how irrational it seems. That has to be me. I'm young and there's no reason I shouldn't get to feel this way for the rest of my life. That's what everyone's chasing, but we're all just so scared. Well, I'm not going to be scared anymore. Deep breaths, Carly.

"Mollie, I like you!" I yell to my empty bedroom.

That felt good to say out loud. I like Mollie Fae. I like her in a way that makes me want to slow dance in the street with her. In a way that makes me dance around to '80s hair band songs alone in my room. In a way that I have to tell her because if I don't, I'm going to lose my mind. I'm not scared anymore. There's a girl out there who I like and who, by some wonderful miraculous coincidence, likes me back. Or liked me back. Semantics. The point is, I'm not done yet and I hope she isn't either.

I learned about this law in my physics class called inertia. Basically, it means that people and things are really lazy. Like when you're watching Netflix and it times out and asks if you're still watching. Having to lift your hand and click Continue Watching feels like the most daunting task in the world. Once you click it though, you think now's a good time to get more Oreos or go to the bathroom. That's inertia. A person or body is going to keep chilling until some force acts on it. That force being the need to go to the bathroom or Netflix making you reevaluate your life or something equally important.

It's a little bit different when it comes to two bodies. Let's pretend they're carts connected by a string. That string can be a metaphor for love or friendship or hate or anything. The point is, they're connected. There's always a force acting outside those bodies that's trying get them to move together. Depending on the stubbornness of the bodies, that can be a lot of effort. That force, though, is going to keep pushing and pushing until it finally overcomes the inertia and the friction and then BOOM. Let there be motion. It's so easy once you start. Believing is so easy once you start.

This kid's still in the fight.

36

She's the One
by Bruce Springsteen

Monday morning comes and I feel like a new woman. I wake up before my alarm and I'm out the door with enough time to go inside Starbucks instead of just driving through. Annie and Todd are shocked to see me at school on time and I'm shocked to see them come in late, looking extraordinarily guilty.

"Class, class! Wow, can you believe this is the last week of your senior year?" Mr. Hall asks as the bell rings. "Lucky for you, we still have a book to finish talking about.

"Who knew we could talk about a short book for this long," Todd groans. Annie pats his arm and smiles.

"So, *Mrs. Dalloway*. What did you think of it?" Mr. Hall asks.

"Boring."

"Stupid."

"Sad."

"Okay, yeah. That's good. Go with that. Why was it

249

sad?" Mr. Hall encourages us.

"Because it's all about time," I say. "I mean, Clarissa talks about the bell tolling so much that Big Ben is basically a character."

"So you think time is inherently sad?" Mr. Hall walks over to my desk.

I think about that for a moment. "No. Not inherently. It can be if you feel like you wasted it or if there's something you want, but can't get."

"Did Clarissa waste her time?"

"In a literal sense, no. She was moving non-stop from the time the book began, but there's that whole thing with Sally and the flower on the terrace," I respond, sitting up straighter. "Almost like the part in *The Great Gatsby* when Jay can choose to kiss Daisy and become mortal, or go up those stairs to immortality. Clarissa didn't want to be interrupted by Peter that evening. She wanted more time, but the constant tolling of Big Ben in the present day proves she has more time, just not in the way she wants. So, yeah, I think time got wasted and before she knew it, she's unhappy and married."

Mr. Hall laughs and walks back to the front of the classroom. "Happens to the best of us."

Maybe I actually did like *Mrs. Dalloway*. I mean, I doubt I'll read it ever again, but I totally relate to kissing a girl on a terrace and equating it to a religious experience. There's that whole time thing too. No matter how much we want it to stop or slow down or speed up, it doesn't. It just ticks on, oblivious to what's going on in our lives.

I don't want to wake up when I'm ninety and wish I'd done something I didn't do. My mom always says having regrets is foolish and that's true. Having regrets just wastes time and energy. Time is the one thing you can't get back. You can win back girlfriends and boyfriends and jobs, but you can't go back if the moment's passed. You just have to make a new moment and fight like hell to make it the moment you want.

Some people say life's like a tunnel, and when you're about to die you can see a bright light at the end of it. I think that's pretty sad. That analogy kind of means we spend most of our lives in a dark tunnel that stretches so far away into the distance we can't even see a hint of light until it's too late.

That blows. I don't want to live my life in sadness and darkness, surrounded by misery until my final moment comes and BOOMSLAM, it all has meaning. That's utter garbage if you ask me. I think life is more like a series of tunnels. Or like driving on a mountain road where you're going in and out of forests and around tight curves, with flashes of light and beautiful scenery along the drive.

Things are shit sometimes. That much is a given for everyone. Even kids who seem to have it all have bad days when their Land Rover has a flat tire and their parents won't let them borrow the BMW. It's universal. But for most of us, the bad stuff comes in waves. Sometimes we have bad days, but sometimes we get to drive the convertible on the Pacific Coast Highway in the sunshine with the perfect soundtrack. Sometimes is surmountable. The point is, I'm pretty confident that everything in my life is going to be okay, even though it's been dark for a little while now.

And I feel like I had some sort of say in this. Inadvertently. I did choose my actions, but I didn't do anything to try and fix the consequences. I tried to let time do all the heavy lifting. This too shall pass. Yeah, it'll pass, but you have to let it. I've just been holding on because living in this funk is so easy.

It's now or never. Fight or flight. One last Hail Mary.

My knee is jumping and my stomach feels sick. Not like vomit sick, just bubbling. You know how your stomach gets right before you get diarrhea? All wild and jumpy? Swirling and spinning. And oh my god, I think I'm going to shit out my heart. Next thing I know, I'm running, pushing my desk out of the way, tripping over Annie's backpack. Mr. Hall is shouting that I need a hall pass, but I dare someone to try and stop me now.

I take the stairs two at a time and round the corner into the main hallway. Past my first-year locker, past the decrepit stuffed lion mascot and into the blistering, blinding sun. I hear the sound of gym classes on the football field as my feet crush the grass. I see everyone playing flag football in their gym uniforms and I see her, ponytail flying. Sun gleaming, blue sky shining, and my mind's made up.

I run to the top of the bleachers and I shout as loud as I can. "Hey!"

A few people turn my way, but I'm unnoticed for the most part.

"Mollie Fae!"

I see her, eyes searching, and I refuse to lose momentum, even though her face droops when she sees me, arms waving.

"Hi."

Mollie crosses her arms, the flag football game forgotten. "Carly, what are you doing here?"

I shrug. "I thought we could talk. It's been a while."

"I know, but I really can't right now," she gestures to the field around her. "I'm in class."

"First, gym is hardly a real class. Second, this can't wait," I say as I start walking down the bleachers. "Look, I've been an idiot."

"You've got that right," I hear Claire say from midway down the field.

"Thanks for the support," I respond, and receive a less than enthusiastic salute in return. "Listen, Mollie. I've been dumb for so many reasons. At that party, I was drunk and lonely and I screwed up royally. You were right to ignore me, but I can't live with that. I can't let this play out without trying one last time. This is really hard to say and I'm just going to keep talking until it finally comes out of my mouth. Just give me a second I'm almost there holy shit I LIKE YOU," I yell, and let out a deep breath. Everyone in the gym class is staring at me. Part of my brain is screaming to run away, but I'm not giving in anymore.

"I like you, Mollie. I spent a long time thinking of every possible worst-case scenario because of my own insecurities. I've been scared and okay living in the worry. That's the main reason I'm an idiot. I should have wanted to embrace this feeling of jumping off a cliff with you, but I was afraid. Now I feel like Icarus and you're the sun. There's such a chance my wax is going to melt and I'm going to spiral to my doom, but I don't care. I like you, Mollie. And I should've said that when you asked me and I'm sorry I didn't, but I'm saying it now. I hope that counts for something."

Silence. I think I hear my wings melting and my chest is heaving. She's standing there and all I can think is that she looks so beautiful. Short, soft cotton shorts, gray t-shirt with a small v-neck cut-out and sweat stains peeking out from under her arms. Dirty white Converse high tops with bunched-up socks. Her cheeks have a slight red tint and her hair's just a little frizzy around her face. I am so, so hopelessly hopeful.

I take another step toward her. "If after all of this you want nothing to do with me, I understand. I just had to try one last time," I say. "But you should know I'm not scared anymore. Well, I mean I am, but for entirely different reasons. Most of which center on the fact that I really want to kiss you again and I'm scared that was a one-time offer."

I see her lips twitch slightly and I pray to every force in the universe that this is a good sign.

"You're an idiot, Carly Allen."

"I am," I say, allowing myself to smile a little. "I'm a total idiot. I should never have done half the things I did, but I did them. So I'm asking for your forgiveness. And dinner," I add. "I'm asking you out to dinner. Oh!" I say, snapping my fingers. "And prom. I'd also like to take you to prom."

"I do love dinner and dancing," Mollie replies, taking a step toward me. "And you do make a compelling case for forgiveness."

My voice wavers. "What do you say? Take a chance on a fool like me?"

Mollie looks at me for a long time, and I hold my breath. I might pass out. She nods slowly, smiling. "I think I'd like that."

It's like a damn movie. Mollie grabs the collar of my

shirt and kisses me. I hear the cheers of the kids in her gym class, but maybe that's all in my head. I feel her hands on my neck and the warm sun on my face and I know it's real. This is what life is like when you believe in yourself.

I truly believe that, no matter what age, if the person you want to kiss wants to kiss you back, you're one of the luckiest people on the planet.

37

What a Wonderful World
by Louis Armstrong

"Okay, and what does the mitochondria do?" I ask, pacing back and forth in front of Claire.

"It's the powerhouse of the cell. Makes it do shit," Claire answers, picking her nails, slumped against the lockers.

"Good, good. Who's considered the father of genetics?"

"Greg," she says.

"You're not on a first-name basis with the father of genetics," I say, exasperated. "What's his last name?"

"Mendel." She finally looks up at me. "Can you stop pacing? You're stressing me out."

"Sorry," I say, sitting down beside her. "I'm just nervous."

"Why the hell are *you* nervous?"

"Secondhand nerves, superstar. I want you to do well."

"Awww. That's the most tutor thing you've ever said to

me."

"Hey, I've been a good tutor! You wouldn't know what to do with an actual tutor."

"Guess we'll find out soon enough," she says, leaning her head back against the lockers.

"You know biology inside out now. All the way down to the cell, which is the building block of...," I say, nudging her shoulder.

"Life." She looks over at me. "Promise I'll be okay?" she asks.

"Promise."

Ms. Bennett opens the door next to me. "Are you ready, Claire?"

I stand up and hold out my hand. "It's now or never, champ."

Claire takes my hand and I pull her up. "I told you, you sound like a ninety-year-old man when you say stuff like champ," she grumbles.

I pull her into a hug. "You'll do great, champ."

She hugs me back, then picks up her bag and starts to walk into the classroom. She turns around and I give her a thumbs up with the goofy grin I know she hates. Claire takes a deep breath and then she's gone. Ms. Bennett closes the door behind her. I'm going to miss that pain in my ass.

I sit down and lean against the lockers. Ever since English class, I can't stop thinking about how time just keeps moving along at the same pace, but it feels like it's always speeding up and slowing down. If you told me that it was only yesterday I'd started high school, I'd believe you. These four years could've just been one crazy night, stretching endlessly in my mind. It's so scary to the do the big things in life. College, dating, graduation, marriage, babies. And sometimes there's a certain comfort in the running and the going and the leaving. I've been swept up in those feelings for four years, and now that I've finally made it to this moment, this precipice, I just don't know how I was so oblivious to the now. The beautiful love affair that happens in front of me every single day.

I guess it all kind of makes sense. Wishing away the days while being afraid of growing old. It's easy to dream about a future that's so much brighter than the present, but once that future comes, you have no idea what to do with it. It's an endless cycle of wishing a stage of your life is over so you can actually, finally, really start your life. Before you know it, you're old and bitter and saying how life's a joke. It's not a joke. The joke is thinking that one part of your life will be more meaningful than any other part of your life. This life is beautiful and I'm sure of that. I wish I didn't worry so many of those days away. Never let me be that foolish again.

It's slowly hitting me that this is it. I'll never be able to slide notes into Annie's locker again, and there are so many janitor's closets I never got to make out in. No more teachers, no more homework. Still dirty looks, though. But no more linoleum or abandoned stairwells or anything. Just the rest of the world. Waiting at the drop-off of an abyss. Whew. That's not fundamentally petrifying or anything.

"School's basically out, Carly. Claire's in her last final. You're pretty much all done. You can turn off that brain of yours now," Ms. Bennett says, as she closes the classroom door quietly behind her.

I smile. "Old habits."

"You mind if I sit next to you?"

I gesture to a spot on the floor. "It would be my honor."

"Ah, you know, Carly, I had my doubts about you," she says when she gets settled.

I laugh. "How so?"

"Well, when you walked into biology your freshman year, you were just a ball of nerves. Even worse than the other kids, but you were so smart. You worked hard on the things that were hard for you and I was so looking forward to watching you open up, but you never did. Not once that whole year. There was something holding you back. I always listened, but the teachers never gossiped about you."

"Wait! Teachers gossip about us?"

She laughs. "Of course. This semester, though, you and Mollie have been quite the topic."

I turn into a tomato, I'm sure of it.

"You have the blessing of all the teachers."

I shake my head. "How do you guys even know about this stuff?"

She raises an eyebrow. "Well for one, you and Mollie frequent the art supply closet as of recently."

"Forget I said anything." I bury my face in my hands. Ms. Bennett just laughs.

"You're a good kid, Carly. I've known that for years, but I'm so glad to have been able to watch you come into your own. The scared little girl you were freshman year has become an intelligent, motivated young woman. That's why I picked you as a tutor. I thought you'd have some insight for the kids."

I smile behind my hands. "Not because of my natural teaching skills?"

She laughs. "Oh, no. You're very smart and talented in many facets of your life, I'm sure, but you were not meant to be a teacher. Not in the traditional sense anyway, but Claire fell in love with you and that rarely happens. It's your ability to be so effortlessly who you are." I look up and she smiles at me, reaching out to touch my arm. "You have such a beautiful life ahead of you. I really hope you keep in touch, but know that I'm not above putting a Google alert on your name."

I feel tears drop to my lips, the sweetest tears I've ever

tasted. "Can I give you a hug?"

"Of course."

It's a little strange to be hugging Ms. Bennett, and we both ignore each other's tears falling onto our shoulders. She's a wonderful teacher and I'm feeling very lucky to have known her.

She pats my shoulder. "It's getting late, Carly. Mollie's probably waiting on you in some supply closet."

I pull myself upright and give her face a really good look. It's red and a little blotchy. She's young. Not as young as me, obviously, but she has lots of years ahead of her. I hope she knows that. I hope she's not like I was. I hope her personal life is filled with love, because some people deserve an extra-beautiful life and she's one of them. She's been rooting for me and I didn't even realize it.

Ms. Bennett smiles one more time before squeezing my shoulder. I watch her leave and know that the sadness I'm feeling will fade.

I see Mollie waiting outside the third floor art room. She's very pretty. I've known that for quite a few years now, but here, on the fourth to last day of school, she's right in front of me and she seems so different. Still as beautiful as the first day I saw her, but sweeter now. She's wearing a light blue summer dress and the sandals from the night we went to the meteor party. I feel so simple. Here's this girl I care so much about, standing in a place that's embedded in me. I'm bursting with love and happiness and fear for the future, but also sadness about saying goodbye to so much.

Simple, really.

Simple because I feel it all and it's wonderful that I'm finally letting myself feel it all. I'm scared and nervous, but now everything's in surround sound, Technicolor, Cinemascope. I'm weightless, like I've just stepped on the moon.

Mollie notices me as I get closer. "Sign my yearbook?"

I kiss her on the cheek. "For you? Anything." I'm eighteen and maybe on some sort of fast track to being in love. It seems like a pretty solid promise to make.

38

Heaven Is a Place on Earth
by Belinda Carlisle

Mollie invites me over to her house under the guise of planning for prom. I don't know much about prom, but I do know that Mollie cares a lot about it and now, consequently, so do I. I've gone shopping with Annie almost every day after school to try and find the right tie to match Mollie's dress. I haven't found shoes yet or picked out a corsage and prom is almost here. This is tough stuff.

Not much prom planning actually gets done because I discover something unimaginable. Mollie Fae has never seen *Clueless*. It's an American treasure. Alicia Silverstone, thank you for helping little Carly Allen realize how gay she was going to be. But seriously, *Clueless* wipes the floor with Quentin Tarantino's entire filmography. Come at me, film snobs.

The credits roll as *Tenderness* by General Public plays on. Mollie looks up at me, all wide-eyed and sparkling. "Are you hungry? I'm hungry. I think there's still some cake in the fridge."

"I'm sorry. You've had cake here this whole time and you didn't tell me?" I ask, pushing her hair behind her ear.

She lets her cheek fall into my palm and I feel the grin, all lazy and sweet, stretch over my face. "Mmmhmm." She presses a kiss into my hand and folds it up tight. "Follow me. Just be quiet so we don't wake my parents up."

Mollie pulls me off the bed and I stumble, legs unsteady. She pushes her bedroom door open ever so slightly, checking to make sure the coast is clear. I'm pressed up right behind her and we're peering out into the deserted hallway like Velma and Daphne. I don't even have to say a gay Velma and Daphne because those two were gay as hell.

Her bare feet pad down the hallway while I slide along the hardwood in my socks. I catch a glimpse of baby photos displayed neatly in frames on the walls. Cute little button nose, tennis-ball-size chubby cheeks, and the same sparkle in her eye.

The kitchen is massive compared to the rest of the house, and the gleaming countertops are an endless sea of granite. I jump on top of one while Mollie opens the biggest fridge I've ever seen, covering both of us in bright yellow light. She bends down a little, scavenging for the promised cake, while I let myself enjoy the really nice sight in front of me. Her sleep boxers are rolled up at the waist and they stop at just about mid-thigh. All I can think about is those legs and how they were tangled up in mine not long ago and that makes me feel like the luckiest fool on the planet.

Mollie turns around and catches the look on my face, but before she can tease me we hear a man's voice.

"Mollie! Is that you in the kitchen?"

I drop to the floor as cat-like as I can, which is nowhere near as smooth as anticipated. My knee bangs at least three drawer handles on the way down, but I manage to curl myself into a ball. I picture Mr. Mollie Fae with a shotgun and imagine that my last moments on earth are going to be in the biggest kitchen this side of Martha Stewart's. I had higher hopes for this moment, in all honesty.

"Yeah, Dad, it's just me," Mollie says, swinging the fridge door open a little wider to block his view of the island counter I'm hiding behind.

"What're you doing out here?" His voice is very close now and I watch Mollie shift her weight and balance with one foot on top of the other.

"Want me to make you a snack?" he asks. I can see the top of his hair over the counter.

"Oh, no, that's okay. I'm just going to find something quick. Got a paper due tomorrow. Last one."

"Well, let me know if you need anything," he says, and leans over the fridge to plant a kiss on the top of her head.

I scoot as far back against the cabinets as humanly possible. Mollie's shoulders tense and she looks at me out of the corner of her eye. I'm not confident either one of us is breathing.

Look, Jesus, I know we don't chat much and I know I take your dad's name in vain a lot and people who really like you condemn my existence, but I'm asking you to get me through this. You seem like a good dude, so I'm asking you, bro-to-bro, to please get me through this.

"Love you, dad," Mollie says.

He ruffles her hair. "Love you too," he says, and takes a few steps back.

Thanks, Jesus. You had me worried there for a second, but you pulled through. You're the realest, most righteous MVP.

"Hi, Carly."

"Hi," I say, then smack my hands over my mouth.

Jesus, what the hell? I thought we were cool! I thought we were on the same page.

Mollie stares at me as her dad leans over the counter. I give him a meek wave and he smiles. "You're as cute as Mollie said you were."

I blush. "Thank you, sir."

He shakes his head and looks at Mollie again. "I'm going to let you two have this one." I see Mollie's shoulders relax. Then he focuses on me. "But this will never, ever happen again."

I nod.

"Good. Mollie, I'll see you in the morning. Carly, I'd better not see you in the morning."

I keep nodding as Mollie's dad leaves the kitchen and goes back to his bedroom. I lean my head back against the cabinets and let out a huge sigh. Mollie's doing the same against the freezer door and I can't help but laugh a little. It's like when people laugh at a funeral, only I'm laughing because there could've been a funeral tonight.

Once my nerves have calmed a bit, I stand up and put my hands on Mollie's hips. I feel her jump a little before she turns around to face me. I take her hands and place one on my shoulder. I leave one of my hands on her hip, half on rolled boxer shorts and half touching smooth skin. Our free hands mix together, fingers clasped.

"Are you really trying to slow dance with me after my dad just caught us in the kitchen at one a.m.?"

I push her hips with mine to get them moving. "That's exactly what I'm doing, and I'd appreciate it if you went along with it."

"Prom is happening soon. Could you not wait until then for our first dance?"

"No. Something about you and the fridge light and the prospect of that cake makes it all too overwhelming," I say as I dip her a little. She holds on tighter.

"It's the boxers, right? My ass looks great in them."

I smile and kiss her because she's not entirely wrong. I wonder if things will always feel this simple. I know money and taxes and rent complicate things, but I hope moments like this will always exist. I hope when I'm 97 I can still slow dance in the kitchen by the light of the fridge, or whatever futuristic contraption will be keeping our food cold then.

Living is such a strange concept. We criticize and complain and say we aren't truly, really living unless we're diving off cliffs in Bali or living every day like it's Coachella. What a stupid, pretentious thing to say. You're breathing, right? Well, that's living. I'm not going to lie and say that if I died tomorrow this would have been enough, because it wouldn't. I want to live and breathe and dance and cry for a hundred more years. Even if I live to be 150, it still won't be enough. But this moment and this person and this life right here are damn good.

"Now," I say, letting my head rest against hers. "About that cake?"

"You objectify my body and now you're going to use me for my baked goods. What kind of girlfriend are you?"

"By that definition, I'd say a pretty mediocre one."

We end up back in her room, cross-legged on the bed with half a chocolate chip torte in front of us. If there turns out to be a heaven on Earth, it just might be sharing a

269

Graul's chocolate chip torte with a pretty girl.

"Listen, I understand that you want some of this cake, but I need you to know that I'm fully capable of crushing the entire thing on my own," I say, scooping off a purple icing flower.

"Do you think that's a marketable skill? Like, is it on your resume?" She laughs a little. "Special Skills: Can eat an entire Graul's chocolate chip torte on my own."

I nod. "It'll show future employers that I'm dedicated to a task once I start."

She shakes her head. "Or it'll show that you're a goofball."

"Dude, so rude! This is a skill I've perfected over many years."

"You cannot call your girlfriend a dude!"

I clutch my chest dramatically. "Is this our first fight?"

She shoves my shoulder and laughs.

"Speaking of dedication, we have to discuss our get out of jail free celebrities," I say, hopping off the bed in search of paper and pens.

"You mean, like three celebrities we can have inconsequential sex with?" she asks.

"Yep," I answer, handing her a piece of paper and a pen.

"Did you do this in all of your previous relationships?"

"Listen, I was blessed enough to be born in the same

time period and in the same universe as Anna Kendrick. If the moment arises, I'll be damned if I can't go through with it because I didn't do something as simple as make a list."

"I honestly have no idea who to put on my list," Mollie says.

"That's such a lie. Everyone has at least one celebrity crush. Who do you think is hot?"

She shrugs. "I like personality more. Being funny is the way to my heart."

"Aw," I say. "You think I'm funny."

Mollie shakes her head. "I never said that. I've told you this before. I only like you for your looks," she says, uncapping her pen with her teeth.

"Okay, I'll take that."

It takes me about five seconds to jot down my list, but Mollie's having a tougher time. While she works on it, I finish the rest of the cake. Maybe I should enter a food eating contest. I shake my head. File that away for another time, Carly.

"Alright," she says, handing me her list.

> People Funner than Carly
> 1. Aubrey Plaza
> 2. Jenny Slate
> 3. Seth Meyers

"Well, first of all, great title. Really nice. Also, it's very clear that you have a type. Not a physical one, but definitely a humor type. Do you want to talk about your crush on the old man?" I ask, pointing to the last name on her list.

"What? He's a very attractive older man. You should hope to age that gracefully. Now, let me see my competition." She pulls the list out of my lap.

Carly's 10 Outta 10 Would Bang List
1. Anna Kendrick
2. N/A
3. N/A

"Well, at least I don't have much competition." Mollie laughs and puts the empty cake tray on the floor. "Come here, you little monogamous cutie pie."

I lie down on my back and she lies next to me, head on my chest. We stay like that for a long time, so long that we both doze off for a little while. I see the clock hit five and I know I should leave. My mom gets up every single day at 5:45 and she's the lightest sleeper in the world. I delicately pull myself out of Mollie's arms. She appears to be the heaviest sleeper in the world. I tear off the bottom of my list and write a note for her to wake up to.

After a quick search, I find my shoes and flip off the bedside lamp, leaving the room illuminated only by the moon. I tuck Mollie in and kiss her forehead one last time before climbing out of the window.

I like driving. If this college thing doesn't work out, maybe I can be a truck driver. There would be long periods of time when I wouldn't have to talk to anyone. A rescue pug named Baguette could ride shotgun with me. My uniform would be gay flannel and dad baseball hats. The women's showers in gas stations are generally pretty clean, probably due to the lack of lady truck drivers. Just me, my pug, and hundreds of thousands of miles of highway, endless playlists, and glowing sunsets. In reality, being a truck driver would be a terrible job for me because I'd stop at every cute coffee shop and all the weird roadside attractions. I'd be fired within a week.

Speaking of endless playlists, though, I hate it when people act all high and mighty and say pop music is the literal garbage of the earth. Humanity can't even agree that evolution is real or that Crocs are terrible, so why would we agree on which type of music is best? The closest we'll ever get is Adele, and even then, my mom's one of those who says she "just doesn't understand what all the fuss is about." Yeah, maybe from a technical standpoint pop music isn't the greatest, but who cares. Pop music is made for times like this. When your heart's full of adolescent lust and your stomach's sugary sweet and you're driving down the highway when it's too early for work and too late for play. This is where pop music is meant to live.

Honestly, though, I could drive forever in the kind of

mood I'm in right now, living here in the car. There have been many nights behind the wheel when I almost turned my back on this town. Tonight feels different. I want to keep going, not because I want to run away, but because I feel endless. I feel like I could go as far as the moon tonight.

I won't leave just yet. I've got a pretty girl sleeping soundly in her bed and parents who'll miss me as much as I claim I won't miss them. I've got a lot of history here, and in a few months I'll be leaving for real. Guess all my big kid dreams of running away and leaving this town in the dust can wait just a little bit longer. And prom's right around the corner. God knows, I can't miss prom.

39

Kiss Me
by Sixpence None the Richer

"Hey, Carly? You getting anywhere with your tie?" Todd asks.

I huff at the mirror. "No. This is like rocket science. You can come out. I'm all dressed."

"Okay," he says, pushing the bathroom door open with his foot. His hands are trying to unknot his tie.

"Men's fashion is so basic in every other instance, and then they throw in ties to make people suffer," I say, starting again.

"Yeah, I'm regretting this bow tie," Todd complains as he walks over to the mirror where I'm standing. He's tall enough that he can stand behind me and still see his reflection.

"I'm gonna yell for my dad," I say.

"I think that's for the best," Todd sighs.

"Hey, Dad! Can you come up here?"

"Be there in a minute, kiddo," his voice echoes through

the house.

While we wait, I walk over to my bed and start putting my shoes on. I think I'm nervous. Am I supposed to be nervous going to prom? I have no reason to be nervous. I asked a pretty girl and she said yes, so that shouldn't make me nervous. Maybe it's because this is really the end. As much as I've wanted it to be here, I don't think I'm ready. I'm scared to move to Oberlin alone. I'm scared to leave Mollie after being together such a short time. Are we going to try to make distance work or just enjoy the summer before we go our separate ways? I don't know if I can bear that.

And Annie. Holy hell will I miss Annie. We've been friends since I marched up to her in kindergarten and said "Your shoes are my favorite color. Will you be my friend?" That was that. Knowing Annie like I do now, I'm sure she was afraid to say no to my friendship proposal. I'm glad she didn't. We'll keep in touch. We have to. I don't think I'd make it without her.

"What do you kids need?" my dad asks, poking his head through the doorway.

"We can't tie our ties," Todd says, holding up his wrinkled bow tie.

"Oh, yeah, I can see that," Dad says, inspecting the bow tie. "Well," he claps his hands together, "let me go get your mother."

"What? You can't tie a tie?" I ask.

"Nope. Never learned. That's why I keep your mother around," he says, walking out of the room.

"Your dad's an interesting man," Todd comments.

"That's an understatement."

My mom makes her way through the door and gasps. "Well, aren't you two just the cutest prom dates!"

Todd stutters and mumbles, "Thank you, ma'am."

"Geez, mom, don't embarrass me," I say.

"Okay, okay. I'll save it until your dates arrive," my mom says as she starts tying Todd's tie. Say that three times fast. "Are you excited?"

Todd nods. "Yes, ma'am."

"You'd better dance with those girls. No one wants to spend all of prom sitting at a table," my mom says, adjusting Todd's bow tie with a final tug.

"Yes, Mother."

"Don't you yes, mother me. Trust me when I say bad things happen when you don't indulge your date in a dance. It's the reason I met your father."

"Wait. Really?"

My mom evens out the ends of my tie. "Mmmhmm. It was a cotillion at the University of Virginia. Cotillion is prom for college kids in the south. I went with this boy from my biology class and he never danced with me. Not one song. All my girlfriends were dancing with their dates and I was sitting at a table listening to my date talk about molecular biology to his dateless friends. On any other given day I would've loved to talk about molecular biology, but it was cotillion and I wanted to dance.

"Then, out of nowhere, your dad showed up in all his hippie glory. Beaded headband, long hair, flower tucked behind his ear. He asked me to dance. Of course this is when my date finally decided to pay attention to me and he said 'Sorry, she's here with me.'"

"What a jerk," I say.

"I looked at him and said 'Not anymore.'"

"Whoa, way to go, Mrs. Allen!" Todd exclaims.

She does a little curtsy. "Thank you very much. Your dad and I danced the whole night and then we went to a Waffle House until I had to go to my eight o'clock class. I went in my cotillion dress and the whole class stared at me. Especially my date. After class, I walked out to find your dad asleep in a chair, with two coffees beside him. That's when I knew I was going to marry him."

I look up at her. "How did I not know that story?"

She kisses my forehead. "You never asked, kiddo."

It's weird to think my parents weren't always parents. It just feels like their life started when they got married and had me. Of course I know that's not true, but it's easy to forget they had real lives. They stayed up late dreaming about somebody, wondering if that somebody was dreaming about them too. They've cried over broken bones and boys and girls and test results. It's easy to forget the people around you are people too.

"Hey, Carly! Todd! I've got some girls down here waiting for you," my dad yells from the bottom of the stairs. Todd and I scramble to put our jackets on and make sure our hair's decent.

My mom straightens my jacket and I'm talking before I even realize it. "I love you, Mom."

A tear forms at the corner of her eye. "I love you too, sweetie," she says. "Now, go get 'em, you two!"

I let Todd walk down the stairs first. We're both carrying corsages. I'm not worried about tripping down the stairs until I see Mollie Fae at the bottom. I grab the handrail and hold on tightly.

She's wearing a strapless mint dress that fits her so nicely. I've watched this scene in a hundred teen movies and made fun of it every time. But now that I'm here, actually in the moment, I understand the hype. *Kiss Me* by Sixpence None the Richer is playing in my head and I feel time slowing almost to a standstill. I wouldn't mind if it stopped right now. I could live forever in this moment.

Mollie Fae smiles at me. My heart kicks up and time moves again. The moment isn't over, but it's moving forward. It won't be forgotten. It's etched in my brain. I like to think there's an art gallery in my brain of freeze frames from my life. Moments that are different from all the others. This is where all the important shots go. The ones you remember with absolute clarity at the drop of a hat. Like meeting Annie, the first time I went to Disney World, learning to ride a bike. All those moments hang in a gallery that I can revisit whenever I want. This moment is the latest, greatest, permanent installation.

"Wow. You clean up pretty nice, Carly Allen," Mollie says when I get to the bottom of the stairs.

"And you look beautiful, Mollie Fae," I respond with a wink.

"I believe this is for you," she says, pulling a boutonniere out of her clutch.

"Wait!" my dad shouts. "Let me get the cameras!"

"Sorry about him," I say to Mollie.

She laughs. "I think it's sweet."

I look over at Todd and Annie. She's wearing a purple dress and Todd's bow tie matches perfectly. She catches me staring.

"You know, you were wearing purple shoes the day we met," I say.

"You getting soft on me, Allen?"

"Don't be an ass," I answer.

She smiles warmly. "Thank you for asking to be my friend."

I will not cry. "Thank you for saying yes."

"You're going to make me cry," Mollie says, looking at the two of us.

"I already cried a little bit," Todd says, and we all laugh.

"I'm back!" My dad arrives with two disposable cameras. He gives one to my mom to take pictures of Todd and Annie.

"Don't just stand there," my mom says, winding the film. "Get to prom-ing!"

The next few hours are a whirlwind of dancing and singing like the carefree youth that we are. Mollie kicks off her heels after the second hour and I take my jacket off right along with her. There's a small food fight between us and Todd and Annie until ice cream falls on my suede boots and Mollie and I rush to the bathroom to try to save them. This leads to us making out for a long time. So long that Annie comes in to make sure we're still alive.

We make it back onto the dance floor and dance until the DJ tells us prom is officially over. The four of us are the last ones to leave. Everyone else is already at after parties getting drunk. We could be there too, but we've all silently agreed we'd rather be here. Now it's midnight and we don't want to go home. We're going to make this night last.

Finally, we pile into the limo and ask to be taken to the Towson Diner. I've been to this place more times than I can count, and it's nice to have this constant when everything else is ending. Our waiter takes a picture of the four of us laughing in the booth.

I can't help but think of my mom's story about her first date with Dad. They probably looked just like us. Delirious, excited, hungry, dressed to the nines, completely alone in a restaurant at two o'clock in the morning. Twenty-ish years later and here I am, living out my own version of that night.

Mollie's telling the story of the night I asked her to the meteor shower party and Todd and Annie are paying rapt attention. I drape my jacket around Mollie's shoulders when I see her shiver, and she leans against me without ever pausing the story.

I think about all the other possibilities that could've been today. Emma could be sitting here, my jacket draped across her shoulders. I could be third wheeling with Annie and Todd. I could be drunk and alone at some after party. I could be sitting at home alone watching *Gilmore Girls,* which I still haven't finished. It could be Annie and me alone in this diner like we've been so many times before. I'm glad it turned out this way. I'm glad this is the possibility that lived to its potential. After everything that's happened, I'm happy. I guess it was in the stars, though. I'm my parents' daughter and history tends to repeat itself.

40

Born to Run
by Bruce Springsteen

"Why do they make the girls wear white?" I ask, swishing around in my graduation robe on the front porch while my parents prep the camera on the tripod.

"What do you mean?" my dad asks.

"I mean think about it. If some poor girl's on her period she's going to be sitting through the entire ceremony stressed that there's going to be blood on her robe when she walks across the stage. That's just wrong. Principal Davis should know that. She was a teenage girl once."

"Maybe not everyone's thinking about periods on graduation day," my dad says, looking through the camera.

"You only say that's because you're a man. All I think about when I see a woman in white pants or a white dress is wow, she's so confident. Like the waitresses at The Cheesecake Factory. If I worked there, I'd call out every month when I was on my period. I couldn't do it. I can barely wear a light wash jean when I'm on my period."

"Is this your way of working through your nerves about your speech?" my mom asks as she comes to stand next to me on the porch.

"No, this is genuinely what's been going on in my brain since I picked up my robe. I'm not nervous about the speech. I'm amazed at my school's lack of foresight. It's like school-sanctioned anxiety."

"Okay, everyone! Pose!" my dad says, scampering over to us as he clicks the shutter and the camera counts down.

"Whew, great photo shoot," I exclaim, taking off the hat after the shutter clicks. "Let's roll."

"Not so fast," my mom says, pulling me back. "We can't have just one graduation photo. This is an important day for all of us."

"Très important," my dad says.

I look over at him. "Since when do you speak French?"

"We all did in the sixties," he shrugs.

"First of all, I feel like that's a lie. Second of all, you were like three in the sixties."

"Pose nicely for a few more photos, then we'll go, okay?" my mom says.

"Fine," I grumble.

****

We're running late because I insisted we stop for coffee at Starbucks. It's the one I went to every morning before school and I figured we should have a full circle moment. Bad idea because the line was out the door. In order to make up for lost time, my dad accelerated wildly out of the parking lot and I spilled coffee on my stupid white graduation robe. Now I'm standing with Annie near the backstage entrance, trying desperately to get the stain out.

"What are people going to think now when they see me?" I sigh dramatically, blotting at the huge spot on my chest.

"Probably the same thing they always think," Annie offers. "I can count on two fingers the number of times you haven't spilled coffee on yourself."

"Really? I'm not that much of a slob."

"The first day of school freshman year and the last day of classes this year," Annie says matter-of-factly. "Every single other day, you've had a coffee stain on your shirt. Sometimes it's big like this one and sometimes it's just a little drop."

I groan. "It's not going to come out is it?"

"Doesn't look like it, no."

"So much for trying to look like a competent young professional."

"Carly, you need to be on stage," one of the tech kids says.

"Any chance you've got an extra robe?" I ask him.

"Nope," he says, unfazed. "Let's go."

"See you afterward?" I ask, turning around to face Annie.

"See you then," she smiles.

The tech kid and I make our way to the stage and I take a seat next to the valedictorian. I can't help but notice that she has no coffee stain on her gown. She probably drank her coffee before putting the gown on. That kind of thinking is the reason I'm not the valedictorian. That and calculus.

I look out at the crowds and watch the families coming in. I smile when I see my parents scouting out the perfect seats. My dad's setting up the tripod to make sure he has a good shot for my speech. The note cards feel sweaty in my hands and I'm worried the sweat is going to wipe the words away. What kind of fool not only makes girls wear white graduation gowns, but also thinks an outdoor graduation in the beginning of summer in Maryland is a good idea? Civilization invented air conditioning for a reason. The valedictorian has her speech in a leather binder. She's really living up to her title.

An announcement is made asking everyone to take their seats, and Principal Davis steps up to the podium.

"Friends, family members, and seniors, welcome to Towson High School's class of 2016 graduation ceremony!"

There are cheers all around as she continues. "I've been principal at this school for thirteen years, and I'm always overwhelmed by the drive and dedication of each new class of seniors. They come to Towson High School as frightened young freshmen who just want to be able to find their way to class without getting lost. By the time they walk across this stage four years later, they've grown into wonderful young adults who sometimes struggle to get to class on time, but not because they can't find the classroom."

Some light laughter from the parents because yeah, we get it, teenagers can be lazy and high school seniors kind of lose their motivation by the end of the year. "I'd like to thank our band and orchestra for being here today to provide the music for this commencement. Ladies and gentlemen, the class of 2016!"

All of us on stage rise as the band plays *Pomp and Circumstance*. Slowly, my classmates make their way across the football field. I see Mollie and give her a little wave as she takes her seat. Todd and Annie are next to each other and they blow me kisses as they sit down. I grab each of their kisses out of the air and tuck them into my pocket. Once everyone's seated, Principal Davis speaks again.

"Each year, the seniors are tasked with selecting a class speaker. The teachers put together a list of students they believe are academically sound and invaluable members of the student body. It's an absolute honor to hold this title, and past winners have gone on to do wonderful things. I have no doubt that the student who won this year will dazzle us in the future.

"This year's student was elected by the largest margin of votes since the creation of the title. She was chosen by teachers who value her hard work and classroom behavior. She excelled as a tutor who worked with freshmen in Ms. Bennett's class. When asked, her peers praised the way she stood up for what she believed in, time after time. This individual has maintained a 3.8 GPA and will continue that work ethic at Oberlin College, where she's been awarded a creative writing scholarship. That's quite a feat for a student who didn't take any of the creative writing classes we offer here," Principal Davis jokes. I can't help but smile a little.

"Without further ado, please welcome your class speaker, Carly Allen."

I stand up to walk to the podium and my legs feel a little wobbly. All of my thoughts are on the coffee stain and how my gown is too long and wondering if it's dragging on the ground. Don't you dare trip, Carly Allen. Principal Davis is smiling at me and I go to shake her hand like we did in rehearsal, but she pulls me into a hug instead. I hug her back tightly and then, after a moment, she lets me go. I take a deep breath and turn to face the crowd. A mix of people I love, people I've genuinely never seen before, and people I never want to see again.

"Good afternoon. First of all, I'd like to thank all of

you for selecting me to be your class speaker, and Principal Davis for giving me that wonderful introduction. I've never heard a class clown described in such an elegant manner," I say, getting a laugh from the audience.

"Second, I'd like to thank my parents. I'm assuming you two did something I should be thankful for at some point in my eighteen years of life. I'm here today, so that's something." I smile.

"Third, thank you to all the teachers who put so much time and effort into getting all of us to this very moment. I'm sure we could've done it without you, but I'm glad we didn't have to.

"Now that those formalities are out of the way, let's talk about what really matters here. Me. Most of you know me for the fine scholarly skills Principal Davis mentioned. Since academia is where I *obviously*, truly thrive, I'm going to use this time to impart some wisdom to my fellow students. It will surely help you in the rigorous college curricula that await you.

"We all have a lot of growing up to do. I still don't really know what a W-2 looks like, how car insurance works is a mystery to me, and I certainly have no clue what I want to be when I grow up. What I do know, for the most part, is that our parents want the best for us, even when they show it by trying to force us to be doctors when we know we're destined to be artists. We're filled to the brim with expectations from our teachers, families, friends, boyfriends, girlfriends, strangers, and ourselves. It's a miracle we're functioning as well as we are, considering all the pressure that's on us. I wish I had a cure for the nervousness and stress we're feeling, or advice that isn't filled with my youthful ignorance.

"However, based on the minimal life experience I have, I can tell you that youthful ignorance is actually our greatest asset. It's what got me here. It's why I'm dating the prettiest, smartest girl I've ever met. It's why I foolishly only applied to one school I could get into, but it's also what got me a scholarship to my dream school. It's why things in my life have worked out the way that they have," I say smiling, looking up from my notes. "So don't grow up tonight or this summer before move-in weekend. I spent four years secretly worrying away high school, trying to fast forward to a fictitious adult promised land I was so sure existed beyond these caps and gowns. Now I'm not sure anymore.

"We have the world at our feet right now, and it's just waiting for us to leave our mark on it. We can be everything our parents wanted us to be and everything they warned us about and everything we've dreamed of. The only thing that's concrete in this world is belief itself. Believing in ourselves, first and foremost. Doors open and opportunity comes knocking when you stop worrying and just trust yourself.

"Okay, so I see some parents out there smiling like they know I've got a lot to learn. And I do. We all do, all you parents included. No one knows everything, and what would life be like if we had it all figured out by the time we were 18 or 35 or even 90? It would be boring. No one in this entire world has any idea what life has in store for them, least of all this graduating class. But whatever comes, I'm certain we'll find all that's bright and beautiful and within our reach. There's magic out there and I, for one, am going to chase after it until the end of time.

"Oh, geez, Principal Davis is shaking her head. If this were the Oscars, I'd be getting played off by the orchestra, but it looks like our orchestra doesn't mind if I keep talking. Okay, I guess I'll wrap this up because I really want my diploma and we've got reservations at Bertucci's for some graduation pizza I do not intend to miss. So, class of 2016, go after the magic. Chase happiness to the ends of the earth. Do it alone or do it with the love of your life by your side. Be young and foolish and passionate and strong," I say with a smile. "Stay classy, guys."

As I take my seat, Principal Davis stands and thanks me for my speech. She introduces the valedictorian, Chrissy Reynolds. I don't really know her. We crossed paths a few times over the years, but we didn't interact much. There's nothing permanent or really worth remembering about her.

She's just been there, our lives lived next to each other for four years. Clearly, school played a slightly larger role in her life than it did in mine, but here we both are. Standing at the finish line of a marathon.

Chrissy is swapping cliché pop song lyrics for even more cliché quotes from Shakespeare. I don't hear a word she's saying. Even if she was telling us all the answers to all the secrets of the world, I wouldn't hear a damn thing. My eyes are searching the rows for Mollie. I finally find her and she's got a tear in her eye, because of course she does. She's totally into the sentimentality of this moment and I love her for it.

Suddenly there's a rush of movement to my right and I see my bandmates hurdling over stadium bleachers, taking the field. Fully nude, streaking just like they'd promised. Claire's standing on her chair near my parents, phone out, yelling at them to slow down so she can get a good shot.

Mollie's throwing her head back now, good old-fashioned laughing. The valedictorian's speech about the future is cut short and that's okay by me. Doesn't she know the future's irrelevant? Spend too much time worrying and wishing away days and before you know it, the moment you were afraid of is long gone and you're still worrying about it, doing nothing. College is happening, yes, life is happening and it's always going to be happening. And I finally feel like I'm ready for it.

I look at Mollie and see my present, and maybe a part of my future. As I catch her eye, she gives me a wink. Security guards on Segways are trying to catch my bandmates, but they're fighting a losing battle. I let myself fall in love with these people and this town and this moment one last time. I'm at home and at ease, finally, with the place that knows me so well. I take a breath, stand on my chair, and let out a scream you could hear on the other side of the Milky Way, then throw my cap high into the air.

Hello, world.

Acknowledgments

Every single time I opened up the document that held the draft of this book, I'd be shocked at the word count. For something called *Garbage*, there sure were a lot of words. And now it's a book, which is weird, wild, and proof that magic is real. In my fifth grade yearbook I said I wanted to be a writer, despite displaying minimal interest in writing at that time. Nevertheless, I hope ten-year-old me is proud.

First, thank you to my mother. Thank you for being my first editor. Even though you refused to adhere to my desire to communicate about the book only through email, I think we made a pretty great team.

To my dad, thank you for marrying a copyeditor. Just kidding! Thank you for being a wonderful dad and encouraging me to follow every single last one of my dreams. From working at Target to being a Disney Cast Member to working at film festivals and, finally, to writing a book. People are going to judge this book by its cover, and thanks to you, I think they'll like what they see. I genuinely can't thank you enough.

To Sunshine, the Steve Carell to my Ryan Gosling circa *Crazy, Stupid, Love*. Thanks, broski, for watching *One Tree Hill* with me that one time.

To all my friends from all over, thank you for being my friend. As simple as the word friend sounds, I'm incredibly lucky that of all the people in all of the world, we found each other. I love each and every one of you. Ugh, feelings, gross. But seriously, y'all are okay.

This book was written in coffee shops in Pittsburgh, Savannah, and Toronto; in classrooms in Towson, Orlando, Roanoke, and Morgantown; in airports in Frankfurt and Los Angeles; on Main Street in Walt Disney World and Disneyland; on a balcony in Cannes; and in a hotel room in Paris. I can only hope that you're reading it in coffee shops, classrooms, airports, hotel rooms, theme parks, and on balconies in all of those places and more. And I hope you're reading it with the love of your life by your side.

ThankyouThankyouThankyouThankyou

Want to be the first to hear about Carly Allen's latest
and greatest adventures? Just send an email to
BurnBeforeReadingBook@gmail.com
and we won't let you miss a thing.

About the Author

Tina Kakadelis is an unemployed ex-student. Although she graduated from the University of Central Florida, she doesn't have a career path, so she's really banking on selling a book or two. Follow her on Twitter for the latest about how pretty she finds Anna Kendrick's face, and for rants about couples on *House Hunters* (@captainameripug). *Burn Before Reading* is her first book.